She Swiped Right into My Heart

By the same author

Few Things Left Unsaid
That's the Way We Met
It Started with a Friend Request
Sorry, You're Not My Type
You're the Password to My Life
You're Trending in My Dreams

She Swiped Right into My Heart

Sudeep nagarkar

RANDOM HOUSE INDIA

Published by Random House India in 2016
1

Copyright © Sudeep Nagarkar 2016

Random House Publishers India Pvt. Ltd
7th Floor, Infinity Tower C, DLF Cyber City
Gurgaon – 122002
Haryana

Random House Group Limited
20 Vauxhall Bridge Road
London SW1V 2SA
United Kingdom

978 81 8400 745 9

This is a work of fiction. Names, characters, places and incidents are either the product of the author's imagination or are used fictitiously and any resemblance to any actual person, living or dead, events or locales is entirely coincidental.

This book is sold subject to the condition that it shall not, by way of trade or otherwise, be lent, resold, hired out, or otherwise circulated without the publisher's prior consent in any form of binding or cover other than that in which it is published and without a similar condition including this condition being imposed on the subsequent purchaser.

Typeset in Adobe Garamond by Manipal Digital Systems, Manipal

Printed at Replika Press Pvt. Ltd, India

A PENGUIN RANDOM HOUSE COMPANY

Prologue

You don't always get to experience your most cherished feelings. You might love rain, but you might end up taking cover under an umbrella when it actually rains. You might crave fame, but end up hiding behind sunglasses once you achieve that fame. Similarly, you might love a person, but many a time, that is not enough. Sometimes, what you love is not what you deserve.

Tushita certainly deserved better in her life. She never felt secure in Andy's arms but she loved him nonetheless. She had almost broken her hostel rules just to be in his company that evening. However, she was scared out of her wits.

'Andy, let's leave. It's not safe to be here.'

'Relax. Nothing's going to happen.'

Tushita was paranoid, and repeatedly requested him to return as she sensed something fishy, but Andy was not in the mood to skip the plan that night.

Prologue

'Just shut up,' Andy screamed, infuriated by Tushita's constant nagging.

Tushita kept mum and quietly walked on Anjuna beach towards Curlies Shack. They had parked their motorbike at a distant corner because no cars or two-wheelers were allowed in the vicinity of the shack. As they inched closer, they could hear heavy trance music playing, and they saw some foreigners smoking and dragging on joints and cigarettes inside the restaurant.

'Can you get me some?' Andy asked the guy behind the counter.

'What?'

'Party pills, dude. MDMA?'

Tushita had a puzzled expression on her face as the guy behind the counter came forward. He looked Nigerian to her. Tushita recollected that she had seen him with Andy once before. The way they exchanged smiles, they seemed to know to each other quite well.

'How much?' Andy asked, brandishing cash from his wallet.

'Half a gram for Rs 3000.'

The deal was locked. He handed over the packet to Andy and added, 'Whenever you need more, just ask for Jack in the restaurant.'

Andy nodded and took Tushita to the dance floor. She was shocked looking at girls her age rolling joints and

Prologue

having such easy access to drugs. That was not the lifestyle she favoured. She wasn't new to smoking and drinking but she always kept drugs at bay.

'You want to try some?' Andy asked Tushita.

Tushita said no, but Andy kept pestering her until she gave in.

'Om Namah Shivaay . . . Om Namah Shivaay . . . Namo Shankar Namah Shivaay . . .' the trippy Bob Marley song played on repeat mode. She was high by the time they started dancing. Slowly, Andy started kissing Tushita's neck, moving down to her shoulders.

'What are you doing?' Tushita resisted.

'I was just trying to make you comfortable.'

'You are making it worse.'

However, she couldn't help but succumb to his advances due to the effect of the drug, and just when they were about to kiss, the atmosphere suddenly turned chaotic. Tushita registered that everyone was running outside the shack manically.

'Andy, just run. We are in trouble,' the Nigerian shouted.

Andy loosened his grip on Tushita's body and ran towards the counter. He exchanged a few words with the Nigerian and disappeared within a fraction of a second. The cops had unexpectedly raided the place. Tushita thought of following Andy but someone stomped hard on

Prologue

her foot, injuring her. Somehow, she managed to enter the washroom nearby. As soon as she closed the door behind her, she heard gunshots and screaming. The gunshots became louder and louder and they continued for quite some time.

'Please help me,' she texted her close friend only to realize that there was no network coverage.

Tushita waited for Andy but there was no sign of him. She thought she had control over her actions but that was not the case. She had been blind. Her friends had warned her about him but she had not listened. She had become the person she had always hated. It seemed like she had sold her soul to him. She felt depressed. She was not weak; she had thought it was love. The bitter truth, however, was that it was not love she felt for him, but fear. This fear had brought her nothing but tears and had taken the place of trust in her heart.

The commotion outside became louder and louder. Horrified, she hid in one corner of the washroom, her eyes tightly shut. She had never heard gunshots before and these alien sounds scared her to bits.

Suddenly, there was complete silence. She thought of moving but she could not muster the courage to move. The next moment, she felt a hand over her shoulder and heard one last gunshot. She froze in fear, and the grip tightened on her shoulder. Her brain froze. A million thoughts then ran through her mind. Was he a cop? Or a drug dealer? Or some stranger who wanted to take advantage of the situation?

As human beings, we have the freedom to choose how to react. Every decision that we make leads us on a different road and has its own significance. The suspicious touch of the stranger made her take a spilt-second decision.

A girl's constant chatter won't irritate you if you really love her. If you give a girl a house, she will give you a home. If you give her groceries, she will make you a meal. If you give her a smile, she'll give you her heart. If you give her your sperm, she will give you a baby. She multiplies and enhances whatever is given to her. So if you give her crap, be ready to receive a ton of shit!

Thank You for Cumming!

'You know what . . . whoever said diamonds are a girl's best friend clearly never owned a bike. Just look at this beauty! Nothing can beat my Thunderbird.' Shibani's face glowed with pride as she admired her bike and strapped on her helmet. They were standing outside the hostel gate.

'So which girl is going to lose tonight?' Tushita enquired.

'Naah. Today a guy will lick my boots,' Shibani boasted.

'Are you serious? You're racing a guy?'

'Good girls sit, bad bitches ride. So just sit and watch.'

Shibani asked Tushita to sit behind her but Tushita made an excuse and moved away. Shibani sped off.

Tushita and Shibani were sisters. Originally from Kolkata, they were pursuing a hotel management degree in

Goa. Shibani was voluptuous and sassy and the protagonist of most men's fantasies. She was extremely fond of bikes and racing and refused to spend hours in front of the mirror. To her, wearing a bra was a symbol of oppression and that shaving oneself was pandering to male pressure. With pierced eyebrows and curly hair, she knew how to carry herself with confidence. She approached socially awkward topics such as sex and lust with an openness that was disarming. She was the kind of girl you could drink beer with on a date and possibly connect on an emotional level but she wouldn't let you get in her pants. She was a feminist who appreciated genuine intelligence and criticized pseudo intellect.

The day's event was the result of a challenge posed by a few boys, just to prove that they were superior. This would not be the first time she was racing, but never before had she raced with boys. However, she was determined to beat them. Wearing a white crop top and black jeggings with knee-length boots, she eagerly walked to the starting point and was ready for the race.

'Show us what you can do. You girls are not meant for racing,' the leader of the gang of boys yelled in a provoking manner.

'What do I get out of it?' Shibani asked.

Another guy leaned forward and whispered something into his ear.

'A date. With any one of us. Your choice.'

'I have a better idea,' Shibani said challenging him.

He looked at Shibani with a raised eyebrow. All eyes were on Shibani.

'If I lose, you get my Thunderbird, but if you lose, I get your bike. Got it, pretty boy?'

Everyone was ready and on their positions. Shibani took out her cell phone to call Geet, her roommate in the hostel, when she heard her voice from behind.

'Bitch, I am already here.'

'Ah hell, get your fine ass here,' Shibani yelled as she opened her arms. 'How do you manage to come out with a Barbified face all the time?'

'Pah-leese, was that all you could come up with?' Geet said, making a face at her.

'Whatever. So you want to do the honours?' Shibani asked Geet with a smile.

Geet, Shibani's best friend and roommate, was a human encyclopedia. Her brain was like a sponge and she somehow remembered all the random stuff she had learned throughout her school life. She was not very popular in college because of her nerdy looks, and hence she was often bullied by her batchmates. She was the kind of person who desired an iPhone, eyed the Samsung S4, read all about Xperia, and finally asked a friend if Micromax was just as good.

She was not bad looking but she did not doll herself up. While most of her shallow friends probably would never watch movies like *Inception* or shows like *Fringe*, she secretly enjoyed them. She was someone who could hold a normal conversation even when she was drunk and dancing on a beach at 3 a.m. Boys used to befriend her frequently, but that was usually because they wanted to get close to Shibani. Geet loved her books and relied on them completely to eliminate any kind of loneliness in her life.

She was simple by nature and felt most comfortable with Shibani and her sister, and the only time she actually opened up a little was during Shibani's bike races or hostel room parties with the people she was familiar with.

Geet took off her shirt. What remained was her crop top with her bra straps starkly visible. She motioned for them to start the engines. Shibani revved her engine a couple of times; the guy followed suit. Neither of the girls bothered to ask his name. It did not matter.

'Ready, get set, GO!' Geet said as she waved her shirt to flag them off. They had to cover a distance of five kilometres and return to the starting point.

Shibani's bike zoomed ahead, leaving a haze of fumes behind. Both competitors were out of everyone's eyesight within seconds. Shibani was a few metres behind but was able to catch up near the roundabout. She increased her speed and was about to reach the checkpoint. She knew she was going to win once she saw the guy in the mirror at some distance trying to catch up. She smiled and made a massive circle creating a screen of smoke. After her victory, she slowly rode towards the gang. Geet was jumping with joy but the look on the faces of all the boys was priceless. Half of them were shocked, their jaws wide open. Shibani walked over to the racer guy as he got down from his bike. He looked really angry and disappointed.

'The ability to speak fluent English is an asset, but the ability to keep your mouth shut is priceless. So from now on, keep your mouth shut in front of us, you jerk,' Shibani said with a victorious expression on her face.

'Whatever. Girls can never beat us boys at anything. They will always be the weaker sex. It was just a matter of luck that you won today, but remember, your luck will run out one day,' said the sore loser.

'That's so typical! Why can't you be a real man and accept defeat humbly? Why is that whenever men of your kind lose to women in any sport, they start badmouthing them? More than your dick, your ego needs constant stroking. Don't try to mess with a girl like me. I will hit you so hard on your balls that you will regret the lack of technology for ball transplantation. We girls are equally strong and independent, so just fuck off.'

Shibani motioned Geet to sit on the bike and, without even waiting for a reaction from the gang of boys, they cruised away like the winners that they were. Some guys think that girls only look for money while choosing a partner. These guys are the ones who only look for cleavage while choosing their partners, not the person's soul. They need someone like Shibani to show them their real worth. Men who understand that women are not just about selfies and shopping but are emotional beings with a depth of intelligence are few and far between.

'Let's take some sandwiches from the Chocolate Room on our way back. I am really hungry,' Geet suggested as they sped towards Vasco Da Gama where their college was located.

'We also have to buy some vodka and beer bottles. We need to celebrate!' Shibani yelled through the helmet.

It was way past their curfew, but it hardly bothered them. A bottle of alcohol for the security guard would help him overlook their transgression. They reached the Chocolate Room, one of the best eateries in town, and ordered a sandwich. Sitting at the table, they were so lost in their conversation that they didn't realize their order was ready a few minutes ago. They went to collect it, when the employee asked them, 'Should I vomit, madam?'

'What?' Shibani gave a confused look.

'Should I vomit, madam?' the employee repeated his question, pointing his finger towards the order.

'Excuse me?' Geet raised her voice when she heard his question properly.

'Madam, should I vomit? Your order?' he repeated yet again.

'Have you lost it? You want to vomit on our order?' Shibani was losing it.

'Madam, aapka order garam karu kya?' the employee clarified in Hindi.

For a moment, Shibani and Geet stared at each other. They tried hard to control their laughter but couldn't. They burst out laughing and it continued for a few minutes. They now realized that he was asking if the sandwich they had ordered needed to be warmed up!

'No. Thanks,' Shibani somehow managed to reply and left the counter.

After collecting the drinks from the wine shop nearby, they headed towards the hostel. They signalled the security guard to open the gate. Shibani had parked the bike outside to avoid sounds that may attract attention. Cautiously, they started walking towards their block when they heard a whisper behind them. For a moment, they were afraid they had been caught sneaking in so late, but soon realized that it was just the guard looking for his promised bribe.

They handed over the bottle and padded softly towards their room and messaged Tushita to open the door. They looked around to ensure no one was watching. As soon as Tushita opened the door, they rushed inside and slammed it shut behind them.

Tushita was watching the popular sitcom *Two and a Half Men* on her almost-dead laptop; she was too lazy to plug in the charger. Shibani hungrily munched on the sandwich they had bought and sighed in relief.

'It feels like heaven. Wow!'

Tushita and Geet looked at each other, and Tushita broke the silence, 'An Indian girl says "I'm in heaven" only when she is in Kashmir or having an orgasm,' Tushita teased.

Tushita was witty and reckless. After her parents' death a few years ago, Shibani had begun to mean the world to her. Their dad's business manager looked after their financial needs. He had worked with their dad since the company's inception, so he was more like a family member.

Tushita was a bit of a misfit. Everyone secretly wanted to be like her or be with a girl like her. She was the perfect mix of the kind of girl that a boy wants to introduce to his mother, and also secretly desires and fantasizes about. She was well aware of her magnetic personality. However, she was completely submissive when it came to her boyfriend, Andy, who hated the bitch-in-heels shade of her personality and always wanted her to be a little Ms Goody Two-shoes. She would always give in to his more dominant personality and, because of that, she was often taken for granted.

Shibani remained silent. Geet took off her T-shirt to cool herself down. Shibani was admiring her body and pouted seductively.

'I am really hungry,' Tushita complained.

'It's not hunger, darling. It's thirst. It's lust,' Shibani added in a mocking, theatrical tone.

'Bitch, please. I am serious. Geet, make Maggi. Remember, hostel life is incomplete without Maggi and porn.' Tushita smirked.

'The induction cooker is not working and we don't have a boiler in this room. How am I supposed to make Maggi?' Geet asked.

'Do something, please.'

Geet placed the noodle cakes in a plastic box. Shibani and Tushita looked on curiously. Geet took the box, went into the bathroom and switched on the geyser. Geet poured some hot water on the Maggi, added the tastemaker, sealed the box, and then dipped the box in a bucket of hot water. She kept a close eye on it for some time; after about ten minutes, she took the box out, opened and stirred it well. She asked Tushita to taste it first.

The familiar aroma made it difficult to resist it. It was the best Maggi she had ever tasted!

'It's simply yummy! I bow to you, Queen of Nerds,' Tushita patted her back.

Geet smiled and added, 'I read about this hack somewhere and see how useful it turned out to be!'

'Okay, okay, don't get carried away now. It's time to drink and chill,' Shibani said and gave a hug to Tushita. 'Baby, I won the race.'

'Superb. But I knew you would win—you always do. Let's celebrate! Vivaan is also going to join us in some time,' Tushita said, opening the beer bottle.

'You've invited him here?' Shibani asked angrily.

'Di, please. He is my friend. Don't overreact; try to go easy on him.'

'I will surely try . . . to go easy . . . and make this night memorable for him,' Shibani added sarcastically.

Vivaan was Tushita's best friend and studied in the same college. He stayed in the boys' hostel. He had become quite close to Tushita and Geet over time. He believed that expecting too much from oneself or the world was bad, as it led to delusions, dejection and disappointment. He was one of those rare friends who would happily accept a candy crush request you sent on Facebook without a single complaint and, what was more, he would never complain about being considered in the 'just friends' category. He respected women because he believed they were equal to men. He did not measure them in terms of their capability to fulfil his desires. Though he had a good physique and a jawline to die for, what made him different was that he genuinely listened to the person talking to him. He was always around when one needed him. He was a modern Renaissance man.

After checking that the warden was not around, Vivaan climbed over the fence of the girls' hostel. He was just about to move forward when he heard voices. He ran into the nearest washroom. The conversation became coherent when the girls entered the washroom, too.

'I just hate this pimple on my face. Tried everything but it's still not disappearing,' one girl said to the other.

'Go without a bra. Nobody will notice your pimple,' the other girl teased.

'Oh, shut up.'

'So, did you make out with him?'

'Who? My boyfriend?'

'Of course, who else?'

'We made love for the first time a couple of days ago. It was heavenly. It's not foreplay if it doesn't end in an orgasm.'

'Did it hurt?'

'Not really. He was gentle with me.'

'Give me some tips on safe sex,' the second girl asked curiously.

'Okay. Write down this tip—remember to lock the doors properly.'

'I wish I had a bigger pair. I should use padded bras more often. At least that will get me noticed.'

'Oh, please. Never do that. Do you feel cheated when you open a packet of Lays and find out that it is only 30 per cent full? That's how guys feel when they unhook a padded bra.'

Vivaan was dumbstruck. He didn't know whether they had come to use the washroom or discuss sexual antics. He messaged Tushita about his condition and she came running immediately after the girls left the washroom.

'Vivaan . . . Vivaan,' Tushita hissed.

'In here.'

Tushita told him to come outside when she realized he was peeing.

'Are you really peeing here? In front of me? Yuck!' Tushita said awkwardly.

'Uhh . . . there is a door in between us,' Vivaan replied.

'I hope you have lifted the toilet seat.'

Vivaan realized that he had not pushed up the seat and hurriedly did so.

'Yes, of course.'

'How do women find things to talk about even in a washroom?' He glanced around after coming out of the stall and added, 'Wow . . . I always wanted to look inside a ladies' washroom.'

As they started walking out, Vivaan casually held her hand.

'Yuck, man. At least wash your hands,' Tushita told him off, wiping her hands against her clothes in a desperate attempt to clean them.

Vivaan felt embarrassed, and quickly washed his hand.

When they entered the room, Geet welcomed him. Tushita gave Shibani a stern look, prompting her to welcome him, even though it was quite a cold and formal welcome. They opened the bottles and sat down. Vivaan excused himself to go to the washroom.

'Do you girls have a face wash? I just want to wash my face,' Vivaan yelled from inside the washroom.

'Sure. I will help you,' Shibani reacted and went inside the washroom.

Tushita and Geet were a little surprised at her helpful reaction. But Geet suddenly understood what was coming next. When Tushita had gone down to fetch Vivaan, Shibani had nipped across to her friend's room next door to get the bottle of 'face wash'. The bottle belonged to her friend's boyfriend who had a filthy habit of storing his semen in it.

'What's wrong?' Tushita asked.

Geet didn't react and Tushita began mixing a drink.

'Take this. Clean & Clear,' Shibani said, handing over the bottle to Vivaan.

'Thanks.'

Vivaan began applying the contents of the bottle on his face. Shibani went back to the room and glanced at Geet, who was staring hard at her, trying not to laugh. Geet could not contain herself any longer and burst out laughing; Shibani joined her. Tushita looked from one to the other, wondering what was so funny. Suddenly, Vivaan came with a wet face complaining that the face wash didn't have enough lather. Both the girls laughed even harder and fell on to the floor. Vivaan realized that something was wrong and took a close look at the bottle. Then he took some of the product out in his palm.

'It's cum!' Vivaan shouted in disgust.

'Thank you for cumming!' Tushita suddenly blurted. Instead of getting annoyed, she had joined in the infectious laughter. Vivaan had been trolled by the girls. He tried to show his annoyance by pretending to charge at them but they were too busy laughing. Shibani teased him by calling him 'facial'. All three girls took pictures of the bottle and shared them with their friends on WhatsApp. Vivaan could not help but get affected by their crazy laughter and eventually joined in. Real friends don't get offended when you abuse or play pranks on them. Vivaan swore at Tushita but it was all in good humour.

There is no better friend than a sister and there are no better sisters than Shibani and Tushita. Geet was always their 'threesome' when it came to playing pranks on others. Three very different people had become the best of friends.

As we grow up, we realize that, though it is important to have friends, it is much more important to have real ones. Shibani was not very fond of Vivaan. She probably didn't like him because he had introduced Tushita to Andy, who was his friend initially. But what she did not know was that it was Vivaan who had saved Tushita during the drugs bust. He accepted all of Shibani's barbs with a smile on his face because of Tushita. You don't need many friends, just a few real ones.

'Drinking four glasses of water is so tough but drinking four glasses of beer is sooooo easy,' Shibani stated.

'Hell, yeah. That's so true. Beer has also helped ugly people get laid since ages,' Geet added.

'Seriously. Andy is a living example. Once Tushita's relationship gets over, she will probably wonder whether she was drunk during the entire relationship,' Shibani added.

Vivaan tried to get up but lost control and fell down. The girls burst out laughing.

'I didn't fall. The floor needed a hug,' Vivaan defended himself and added, 'Tushita loves Andy. She really does. But—'

Shibani stopped him and added, 'Haven't you heard about love quotes? If you love someone you should set them free.'

'Yes, correct,' Geet added and continued, 'If they don't come back, call them up later when you are drunk.'

After everyone had had enough to drink, they decided to play a game of beer pong. 'I am sure you all have played beer pong but this one has a couple of very naughty twists. The first twist in this game is that there are dares placed underneath the cups. Fill up the cups halfway with whatever alcohol you want and place the cups in a triangle formation on the mat. Next, take turns trying to land ping-pong balls in your opponent's cup. If the ball lands in the cup, your opponent has to gulp down a drink and has to perform whatever dare is under the cup,' Shibani explained the rules of the game.

'That's just one,' Tushita pointed out.

'The other twist is that this is also a game of strip beer pong. So, the person who performs the dare has to take off one piece of clothing each time he or she performs the dare.'

Shibani got busy and made dare sheets that were to be kept under the drinks. She arranged the cups quite quickly, too. Tushita and Geet seemed thrilled but Vivaan looked lost. If he lost, he would have to strip in front of three teasing girls. After having lathered his face with cum, he was trying to be careful. 'I don't want to play this stupid game,' Vivaan muttered.

'What the fuck, dude. Where on the earth would you get a chance to see three girls stripping together in front of you?' Tushita asked.

Though not fully convinced, Vivaan went along with it and the game began. Geet rubbed her hands together in excitement. The ball was thrown and it went straight into the cup in front of Tushita. Tushita performed the task, removed her pink top and was now in a fancy black lacy bra. She saw Vivaan glance down at her body quickly before looking away. It was Vivaan's turn next; he removed his T-shirt to show off his well-toned arms. Shibani simply removed her white socks when her turn came. Each one performed the task given to them before the ritual of removing an item of clothing. Geet was winning so far because she was fully clothed, but her luck finally ran out. She picked up her dare sheet from under the glass and read out loud, 'Kiss someone's neck seductively.'

'What the fuck? That's not done!' she protested.

'Be a sport. Just do it,' Tushita urged her.

'I will kiss Shibani,' Geet declared.

Shibani looked shocked when she heard Geet. There was a sense of excitement in the room as Geet and Shibani came face-to-face. Shibani could feel Geet's breath on her as she came closer to her neck. Suddenly, she grabbed hold of her and, instead of a soft and sensuous kiss, bit her hard.

'Ouuuch. You bitch. I will kill you,' Shibani lashed out in pain.

Everyone laughed loudly to show their appreciation of how Geet had turned the dare around. As the game continued, Geet was dressed now only in shorts that barely covered her thighs, and a semi-transparent bra. Tushita was in her black lacy bra and a sporty bikini bottom which looked ravishing on her. Vivaan tried his best to keep his eyes off her but couldn't help himself. He kept glancing at her when no one was looking. Shibani had just a long top on. Vivaan was down to his boxers, and Geet kept staring at his model-like physique. It was the last round of the day and the ball went straight into Vivaan's glass.

'Damn, not me again,' he sighed and picked up the sheet from under the glass.

'Remove everything from your pockets and hang your underpants outside the warden's room.'

He couldn't believe it. He looked at Shibani who already had a wicked smile on her face. Tushita stared back at him blankly while Geet looked tensed. Everyone was already so tipsy that they were not even able to walk properly. Vivaan was scared not only because he had to hang his underpants outside the warden's room but because he had to remove everything that was in his pocket and he remembered a packet of condoms that was in there.

'Go on, dude. The game is on! It's the climax,' Shibani coaxed him.

Vivaan went into the washroom to remove his underpants. When he came out, he emptied his pockets, and out came the packet of condoms. This moment, which was so embarrassing for him, had turned into something hilarious for the girls, who asked him how many a day he went through.

Vivaan tried to defend himself by saying, 'Just a precaution, if ever needed. We live in hope.'

'Dude, using a condom is the first step towards humanity. Second step is to not enjoy it with multiple people,' Tushita added.

Shibani pushed him to proceed with the task. She could not resist humiliating him a little more. She snatched the packet of condoms from him and opened it. Removing one condom from it, she went inside the washroom where the special face wash was kept. She stretched the condom a bit and filled it with the contents of the face wash.

'Now, it's complete. Keep this inside your underwear when you hang it on the door,' Shibani ordered.

'Di, that's too much.' Tushita tried to help Vivaan out.

Vivaan accepted the task as a part of the game and started walking outside. This time he was more fearless because he was too drunk to care. All the three girls started walking behind him with the same air of nonchalance. After covering a little distance, Vivaan lost his balance and fell down, but managed to hold on to the condom and his underwear.

'You know, I'd love to meet the people who say true friends pick you up when you fall . . . mine just laugh,' Vivaan said sarcastically as he smiled at their obvious mirth.

You really don't know how weird your friends are until you get drunk together. There is not much information about the UFO these friends came in, but they surely do belong to some other planet. They reached the warden's room which was on the ground floor and checked if the guard was asleep as usual. After making sure that there was no one around, Vivaan slowly tried to hang his underpants on the lock of the door. Despite being so obviously drunk, he somehow managed to do it. Except for the corridor lights, there was a complete blackout around the campus. 'Dare to dare me again. I should take part in the auditions of the next *Roadies* season,' Vivaan said proudly, folding his hands.

'Well done, dude. Now I accept that you are a man.' Shibani smiled.

'Are you leaving your underwear here?' Tushita added.

'It's going to be of no use to the warden. I hope it does not stink,' Geet concluded.

Everyone made disgusting faces but Vivaan stood there like a warrior who had just won a major victory. Before he could enjoy his victory any more, they heard a sound from inside the warden's room. All of them panicked. They rushed towards their room. Vivaan, however, ran towards the gate and tried to cross over. Before he could disappear in the dark, the warden opened the door wide and saw someone jumping over the gate. She shouted for the security guard and moved forward only to step on the underwear and condom that had fallen down when she had opened the door. She looked down to see the white sticky fluid underneath her feet and sensed what it was.

'Securittttyyyyyyyy . . . Securitttyyyyyyy! What the hell is happening here?' she literally roared in anger.

By then, everyone had disappeared. Vivaan sent a WhatsApp to the girls that he had managed to escape: *Border crossed successfully . . . without leaving any ID proof.* ☺

Mission accomplished. Over and out, Shibani replied.

Even the girls had managed to reach their rooms without getting caught. The nights we don't remember make for the best stories. Everyone was hung over the next day, and while discussing the events of the day before, they realized how they had done ridiculous things and got away unscathed. Tushita and Geet apologized to Vivaan for being a bit too harsh on him during the game but he was a good sport about it. They say friends are like underwear—always near you; but good friends are like condoms—always protecting you. However, Vivaan, Tushita, Geet and Shibani were like Viagra—they lifted each other up when they were down.

The Freak

'I am late. Of course. I am the kind of girl who has a perennial flow of bad luck 24/7,' Geet said, in a dark mood.

'You know, statistics say that everybody has their share of bad luck.' Shibani tried to help.

'Statistics are always wrong in my case. I am an exception,' Geet countered.

Shibani and Tushita were skipping the first lecture for no reason. Within the next few minutes Geet got ready for college, not even bothering to look into the mirror on her way out.

Why should a freak care how she looks?—that is what Geet thought whenever she had to go to college. She was an unpopular girl, hardly noticed. She felt unwanted and depressed.

'Geet, you are late,' the professor said as she entered the classroom. She muttered an excuse and walked inside.

As she walked on the aisle between the benches, her classmates purposely stuck their feet out. She carefully stepped over the feet that tried to trip her. It happened so often that this was now a reflex action for her. As soon as she sat down, she felt a piece of paper embedding itself in her messy hair. She ignored the spitball; she had gotten used to them. But that didn't mean she wasn't annoyed every time she came across a soggy ball of paper in hair. She spent hours in the college washroom picking them out. Whenever Shibani was not around, she faced such humiliation. It had started happening so often that she now believed that this was going to be her life in college. The life of a freak. She was a very different person when Tushita and Shibani were around. Being the butt of jokes and the constant ragging had chipped away at her confidence.

'Are you coming for the next lecture?' Geet messaged both the girls. They both assured her that they would be there during the break.

She regretted coming to college as the backbenchers were continuously throwing spitballs at her. The lecture got over and all the backbenchers declared that they would mass bunk.

'None of you should be seen near the class,' a guy announced, as if declaring an official holiday.

Everyone happily obliged since no one was really interested in sitting through the boring lectures. But Geet was just passing by the corridor when the professor saw her.

'Geet. Where are you going? Come inside,' the professor ordered.

'Damn!' She realized that this would be another reason the students would mess with her again. Sensing the mass bunk, the professor was furious. He decided to mark Geet as present and everyone else absent, so that it would reflect on the record. Without teaching a word, he left. Geet cursed herself for getting caught and her belief about bad luck in college was now confirmed. Just the previous night, she had escaped the hostel warden's ire after the condom incident, but today she was having trouble escaping a mere mass bunk! Someone or other always gets caught but it was just her luck that she was the chosen one. Unsurprisingly, everyone abused her once the professor left for the staff room, 'You ugly thing, if your life is so boring then go and die somewhere; stop sitting for lectures when there is a mass bunk!'

Each time they stabbed Geet with their hurtful words, waves of negative feelings swamped her. Her agony was indescribable. Was it hatred or lack of self-esteem? Whenever she entered college, she felt like a person who had no hopes and destiny. Her sense of self-worth was close to zero.

'Geet,' a voice echoed inside the library.

She jumped in her seat, surprised. The book *To Kill a Mockingbird* fell from her hands and landed with a thud on the floor.

'That was the third time I called out your name,' he said, playing with his mobile.

'Uh . . . really?' she asked, as he bent to pick up her book.

'Rudra. My name is Rudra.'

Rudra was the most popular boy of the college and he was filthy rich. His stubble made him look rugged and intense. He was a mixture of Joe Manganiello and Paul Walker. He was the kind of guy who effortlessly swept any girl off her feet, yet he believed that true love was the kind of love in which the guy never let the kohl of the girl get smudged due to the tears he may have caused. He was the perfect combination of good looks and sensitivity. His confidence was such that it did not stem from his money and the girls around him. It was solely his. Geet could not believe that he was talking to her.

'Do you want it or not?' Rudra asked, holding out the book.

She snapped out of her daze and reached for the book, but before she could take it, he started flipping through the pages.

This always happens. People take my books, and the next thing I know, they're in the trash or I find gum on its pages once they hand it back or . . .

'Ae-tu-cuss?' Rudra tried to pronounce.

'Atticus,' Geet corrected him instinctively and reached for the book again but he held it back.

'What's an Atticus?'

'He's one of the characters,' Geet said. Rudra handed the book back.

She searched for the page where she had stopped reading.

'You're Shibani's friend, right?'

Geet looked up. Rudra was still standing there. Now she understood why he was here. For Shibani. He was just trying to break the ice so that he could come directly to the point.

'Yeah.' She looked back down and turned another page.

'Found it,' she said.

'What?'

'Nothing.' She said and continued reading.

'Men's stiff collars wilted by nine in the morning. Ladies bathed before noon, after their three o'clock . . .'

'Is she in college now?'

Why would he want to know about Shibani? Geet thought and glanced up once again.

'She is about to reach,' she said out loud.

'After their three o' clock . . .'

'What time?'

'Within an hour.' Geet tried not to get irritated.

'I want to meet her.' Rudra grinned. 'Will you introduce me to her?'

Rudra poked her in the back of her neck with his mobile and she tried not to scream in frustration. She was still trying to read the same sentence.

'Why don't you just go and talk to her directly? I am not her assistant.'

Geet shut the book in anger and got up to leave the library. It was not the first time someone was befriending her so that she could introduce him to Shibani. The more she met such people, the more she wished she didn't know them. She may have become thick-skinned but she was human, too. All she needed was a little attention, but no one seemed to care about her other than her two friends.

She tried to console herself. She knew that Tushita and Shibani meant the world to her. Men would come, and men would go, but these two would stay forever.

The three girls were sitting on the last bench waiting desperately for the class to get over. Professor Allen was talking mostly to himself since the students were engrossed in talking to each other. With nothing better to do and bored out of her wits, Geet started taking notes seriously. Tushita was snoring while Shibani was busy with her mobile. Vivaan was sitting with the other guys and was busy refreshing his Facebook account to see if he had received any notifications for the new profile picture he had put. Geet had written two full pages of actual notes when her concentration drifted and she started penning down the lyrics of her favourite song '7 Things' by Miley Cyrus.

Suddenly, she heard the sweetest announcement: 'That's it for today, class. See you next week.'

Tushita woke up all of a sudden from her deep slumber. They were waiting for sir to walk out but he seemed to have other plans.

'Can someone please get up and summarize what we learnt today?' he asked.

The students gazed keenly at their desks waiting for Professor Allen to give up. Unfortunately, he happened to know Tushita's name. Geet couldn't control her laughter while Shibani looked desperately at her notes. Tushita did not even know what class was going on. She got up and gave him an apologetic look, hoping he would let go, but he was stubborn and even suggested she read from her notes. Tushita stared blankly at her notebook that was filled with modern art drawings.

'Geet, at least pass your notes and stop laughing,' she muttered.

Geet passed her notes after letting her get embarrassed for a few minutes. Relieved, Tushita started reading out what Geet had written.

As she approached the end of the second page, Geet whispered, 'That's enough. Don't turn the page.'

But Tushita couldn't hear her, and turned the page and kept reading:

'I probably shouldn't say this, but at times I get so scared when I think about the previous relationship we've shared. It was awesome but we lost it—' She stopped abruptly when she finally realized that the notes were not related to the lecture any more. Everyone sitting in the classroom burst out laughing. But the professor somehow missed the song she had read and was not happy with the commotion at the back.

'She is doing fine. Why are you people disturbing her? Sit down,' the professor said angrily and added, 'Geet, you stand up and continue.'

Dammit! she thought as her luck theory proved right once again. She stood clueless, having no idea of what to say. Shibani and Tushita were giggling beside her. All she thought was how life is unfair all the time. Finally, the professor gave up, but not before telling her to report to his office before the day ended.

Shibani knew exactly what professor Allen did when he called girls to his office. His poor reputation in the college was known to all. However, no action was taken against him since no one ever spoke in unity to the committee board. Shibani knew Geet would be helpless once she entered the cabin. As they walked through the campus, Shibani gave it a shot.

'Hey you, Professor Allen. Stop right there.'

'Are you out of your mind? Is this the way to behave with your professor?' Professor Allen shouted as he saw Shibani almost pouncing on him.

'So, Mr Allen, you think this is the way to behave with your students? Taking them inside the cabin and treating them like your slaves? You moron. You think girls are weak and won't dare to speak a word against you, right? You think that you can continue to show that, as a man, you have the authority to treat women the way you want. I just wish your dad had used condoms properly, then you wouldn't have existed.'

'How dare you—'

'Don't try to scare me. Everyone standing here knows what kind of a person you are,' Shibani yelled, pointing at the people standing around them.

'Your erection is temporary, but my words are a permanent stamp on your character. If boobs could talk, you would have been an awesome conversationalist. You have mistreated girls thinking you can get away with it, but we are not pants that you can pull down whenever you want.'

Shibani continued bashing him with her words until the principal and other higher authorities interrupted.

'Sir, he has tried his cheap tricks on me, too,' one of the girls standing there said to the principal in support of Shibani.

'Yes, sir, With me too,' one more girl added.

Professor Allen got what he deserved. He was expelled not only from college, but was permanently blacklisted as a professor so he couldn't get a job anywhere else. Everyone appreciated Shibani and they called for a party in the evening to celebrate taking a stand against a professor who had always abused his position. Rudra seemed the most impressed with Shibani, which was evident from the way he kept gazing at her without blinking. He was desperately looking for a reason to talk to her.

'Where did you get your clothes from, the trash bin?' a popular girl from the college mocked her in an annoying, high-pitched voice.

The party had just begun and all her friends were busy with something or the other. Shibani was talking to someone about the professor while Tushita and Vivaan were busy drinking. Geet had excused herself to go to the washroom, where she met the gang of popular girls from college. Geet was trying her best to ignore the nasty girl but it wasn't working. As Geet walked past, the girl who had taunted her earlier stuck her foot out, and before Geet could realize it, she had tripped over and landed flat on her face. Some people standing a short distance away laughed at this.

'Fuck off, you whore,' Geet muttered, trying to save face, and went towards the washroom.

'You will always remain single because guys don't want to be around such a dumbass.'

Geet locked the washroom door and tried not to sob. She felt terrible. She wished college meant spending time only in the hostel as she always had a lot of fun there with her two best friends. She faced insults and humiliation at college every day. She wanted to disappear into the darkness and cry alone. She wanted to put an end to all this. She was neither a freak nor a loser. Yet, at that moment, she desperately needed a push to gain her confidence back. Loneliness was the worst. You can have all the money in the world, but if you have no one to share it with, then it is as good as not having it. She washed her face to try and pull herself together, glad that the group of mean girls had left. She went towards the bar and drank five vodka shots in succession. She was so angry with the way she had been treated that she looked for solace in the drinks. It was not that Shibani and Tushita wouldn't have helped her if they knew what was going on, but she never expressed such things in front of them. Geet walked purposefully to the gang of popular girls and noticed that they were discussing a boy they had a crush on.

'Well, I heard you guys talking about boyfriends. So I just realized that maybe I know the guy you have been discussing, or well, at least my boyfriend knows him. If I am bothering you guys, I'll leave.'

Geet spoke with authority and pretended to a have a boyfriend. She pushed her hair back and smiled, as all of them gasped as they took in the news. They were all sharing this look, deciding whether to accept it or not. Geet, however, was sure she had fooled all of them because they looked shocked and hopeful at the same time.

'Wait, teach us your way. How could a loser like you score a boyfriend?' one of the girls asked, her voice shaking in excitement.

Through her drunken haze, she realized that those girls didn't have boyfriends either! *Has it made me susceptible to being exposed in front of the entire college tomorrow?*

'Don't fall for her tricks. She is just faking it,' one girl tried to call Geet's bluff.

Geet tried her best not to show any form of weakness. The girl's analytical gaze pierced Geet like a needle, pinning her down with its invisible strength.

'Wait, this can easily be confirmed . . . show us his picture,' the first girl added.

Geet didn't give up, and instead said something that blew them away. She had read this line in a book where the protagonist was facing a similar fake-boyfriend crisis: 'Tone your mind sexy, curves can wait.'

The trio—Tushita, Shibani, Vivaan—and everyone else at the party were shocked when she revealed that she had a boyfriend. Geet excused herself from the party saying that she had a date with her boyfriend. Looking at the sudden respect showered on her by everyone, she didn't dare to reveal the truth even to the trio; she just walked out. She could now see herself in the world where no one was commenting on her clothes, where she could roam freely in the campus and look straight into the eyes of the people without fearing their taunts. This lie guaranteed that she would assume a new status that would ensure her popularity. She had a nagging feeling that she would regret this lie someday, but as of now, she didn't want to let it go. She loved her 'fake boyfriend' who had suddenly earned her a tad of respect.

You Hurt Me, Are You Happy Now?

A new chapter had begun for Geet. Though the roots were weak, her popularity seemed to have flowered. Suddenly, everyone had begun paying attention to her, and her imaginary boyfriend had already gained a lot of popularity within hours. When she reached the classroom the next morning, she was amazed to see that no spitballs came her way. On the contrary, she was welcomed warmly. In between classes, her classmates wanted to know more about her boyfriend and her date the previous night.

'Have you kissed him?' a group of girls asked in chorus.

'Yes. More than a kiss . . .' Geet smiled, as if remembering the passionate encounter.

'Really? Did you . . .'

'Yes. Last night. I am no longer a virgin.' Geet blushed.

'Wow! I just can't believe it! How did it feel? Did it hurt?'

'Not really. A bit in the beginning, but then it was all about moans and pleasure. He is really good in bed. Gentle, yet wild. The perfect lover!'

'Which flavour of condom did he use?' One of the girls was keen to know.

'Kesar pista.' Geet laughed and added, 'How does it matter? Now please let me concentrate on the lecture.'

Tushita, who was sitting beside her, was staring at her. She just couldn't accept the fact that Geet had kept such a big thing hidden from her and Shibani.

'You never told us! I should have been the first to know that you have a boyfriend *and* that you lost your virginity. It's not fair!' she complained.

Geet simply blushed to avoid complications. All of a sudden, college seemed interesting. She had not realized that the mere news of losing one's virginity could win her the attention she craved. In the last few hours of her life, she had not only made up a boyfriend but had also managed to lose her virginity to him. Talking, discussing and gossiping about him during the lectures made her feel his presence more. She pretended to speak to him and text him, and if that wasn't enough, she even smiled at the screen pretending to read some sweet message sent by her dearly beloved. She was aware that one day the bubble would burst; but what she feared most was that she had begun to feel as if her fake boyfriend was real, even though she knew that he didn't exist. Geet's imaginary boyfriend had started taking control of her life.

What happens when the one who used to take all your pain away is now the one causing it? It's never easy to get over a relationship when you have given up everything to hold on to it. Tushita tried so hard to stop caring, loving and thinking about Andy but she couldn't help herself. Catching up with Geet and Vivaan in the college canteen, she was expressing the pain she was going through.

'You love him, but he doesn't realize it. What's the point of holding on to him if he is just pushing you away?' Vivaan said.

'I agree with Vivaan. You should reconsider your decision to meet him once again,' Geet added.

'It's never easy.'

Geet reminded her of all those times when she had suffered a lot. Andy used to hit her badly just to hurt her. Whenever he became overly possessive and was under the influence of drugs, his behaviour went from bad to worse, bordering on the inhumane.

'You should accept that you have wasted a good part of your life loving someone who doesn't even care.' Vivaan was trying his best to make her understand.

'How can you continue to stay with a person who is not just perennially high on drugs but also hits you, shatters your confidence and doesn't think twice before physically hurting you? You can't ruin your life because it's not easy to get over him. You have to try harder!' Geet reacted furiously.

'You never told us that you are with someone. You should have at least told us.' Tushita tried to put Geet on the back foot while wiping her tears.

'This isn't about me . . . we can discuss that later. The point here is that you just have to flatly refuse if he ever asks to meet you again. Shibani is completely right in hating him. He doesn't deserve anybody's love. Certainly not yours.' Geet expertly shifted the focus from her fake boyfriend.

Tushita didn't react for some time and said, 'One more thing that worries me is Shibani's hatred for Vivaan. Whenever I am around, she pretends to be sweet to him, but otherwise she hates him to the core because he introduced me to Andy.'

'You don't worry about it. That can be taken care of. I don't take her pranks seriously because I know she cares for you. In her place, I would have reacted similarly. After all,

I was Andy's friend first and then yours, or at least that is what she thinks.'

'But that's not true. Yes, we met because of him, but he isn't the reason we are sitting together now. It's because we are friends.'

'Just listen to what your friends are saying and shut him out forever.' Vivaan had a logical solution.

People and feelings change. That doesn't mean that the love once shared by them wasn't true. It simply means that sometimes when people grow, they also grow apart. Shibani was never in favour of Tushita's relationship. Vivaan and Geet were also trying to explain to her about her own worth. The irony was that she was not even interested in continuing the relationship, but was having a hard time getting over Andy. You get used to the presence of that person in your life to such an extent that you cannot imagine life without them. Everything around her reminded her of him. It felt like there was a projector screening a never-ending show in slow motion. Those who knew her admired her dazzling smile and warm personality; they had no idea about the abusive relationship she was hiding.

Geet and Vivaan soon had to leave to attend a lecture, but Tushita didn't move an inch. She had made up her mind—she would meet Andy one last time. Absent-mindedly, she flipped through the pages of her notebook until she came across the lines she had once scribbled:

Her perfect tan skin always amuses,
She chooses clothes that will hide the bruises.
Walking down the street with unbeatable grace,
No one knows the torture she has to face.
She watches the clock with a sad, broken face,
When someone approaches, the smile is back in place.

When she meets him, it is impossible to smile,
He breaks her body and spirit in such a violent style.
Her eyes start watering, knowing what is to come,
Just imagining the bloody mess she was to become.

He lays her down and the painful sting returns,
No matter how many times it happens, it still burns.
It continues for hours, then it comes to an end,
She wakes up the next morning, sore, ready to pretend
That she is perfect, that she is okay.

Putting on her make-up, she fixes herself,
Her trademark smile is back in place.
The sadness is blocked away from her face,
She feels she could collapse under the strain,
She heads out the door, repeating the cycle again.

'Andy, I don't love you any more but I am unable to move on. I am not sure whether we should really continue our relationship. I think we should take a break. I am only willing to consider resuming our relationship if you promise to stop using drugs,' Tushita said.

'Don't even dare to think like that. I know why you are uttering this rubbish. It's because of that Vivaan. You are falling in love with him. Am I right, you slut?' Andy smashed his hand on the table.

Andy's reaction scared Tushita. She could see the anger in his eyes, and knowing how violent he could get, she was terrified. Despite her friends warning her multiple times, she had chosen to meet Andy. She was filled with a sense of dread. She had made a mistake in coming here. The evening at Calangute beach did not feel normal, and neither did the breeze soothe her. There were people around who were enjoying with their loved ones, but Tushita just wanted to leave the place. She tried to explain to him in every way she could but Andy could not accept that Tushita was not the same girl any more.

'Have you slept with him? How many times?' Andy asked, smoking his fifth cigarette in a row.

'How can you even think like that? I don't want to talk to you any more. Let's leave.' Tushita stood up but Andy tugged at her hand so fiercely that she fell down on the sand.

She winced in pain. Andy bent down, not to help her but to slap her hard across her cheek. Tushita was shattered at this turn of events, but somehow managed to wipe her tears and get up. She started walking away but once again Andy pulled her back and used the cigarette butt to scald her arm in several places.

'Please leave me . . . please.'

That was all Tushita managed to utter because of the tremendous pain she was in. He kept burning her with the cigarette until the butt was extinguished. Suddenly, he realized the extent of what he had done and began kissing her burnt skin, as if to make up for the horror he had just inflicted upon her. All Tushita wanted was to run! She began to walk and Andy didn't try to stop her this time. As they headed in the direction of the car park, he pretended as if nothing out of the ordinary had taken place. He smiled at her as he helped her on to the bike.

'Are you okay now?' Andy asked, looking at her through the rear-view mirror.

Tushita just nodded. She couldn't trust herself to speak. As she looked at his reflection in the mirror, she just thought about all the pain he had caused her . . . she realized now that her friends had been right all along, and it was time to say goodbye to the love of her life.

'Let's end it,' she said with finality.

'Please don't start again.'

'I am serious. Let's just end it. Stop the bike and let me get down here. I can't take your torture any more,' she yelled.

Andy could not believe that Tushita could raise her voice and scream at him—or that she was breaking up with him. He pushed her back with all his might without even slowing down the bike. He sped off without turning back after tossing Tushita like a piece of garbage. Tushita was flung through the air and, as she fell on the ground, her head hit a large, and jagged stone jutting out of the road, and she rolled over a few times like a rag doll. Moments after the impact, she went into shock. Dazed and disoriented, she lay motionless, feeling a wet trickle of blood running down from her skull. She tried to get up, not knowing the extent of her injuries. She felt a stinging pain from her waist till the end of her leg. After few seconds, she blacked out, but not before thinking of her friends and her sister who would be left alone in the world if something were to happen to her. She thought someone was trying to pick her up; she heard someone shouting, 'Call the ambulance. She is in trouble.'

Was it too late?

Broken Trust Is Like Lost Virginity

Trust, once broken, is almost impossible to repair. Tushita's heart was well and truly broken by Andy's abuse, and the final straw had been the way he literally dumped her on the road. Instead of his warm arms, she was now enveloped in her own blood as she was taken to the hospital in an ambulance. The oxygen mask had been strapped on to her face. She blacked out, and then suddenly her heart stopped too. The reading on the portable ECG machine had flatlined.

After a few hours, Tushita opened her eyes in an ICU, and she saw Shibani and Geet in front of her, along with the manager who handled her dad's business. Everyone was sad and depressed. Little did Tushita know that the doctors had told them that there was a good chance she would not survive the operation because she had lost so much blood, and because they had to revive her heart once already.

'Please don't die again. We cannot live without you. We had lost all hope. You mean the world to us. Please.' Geet sobbed, holding Tushita's hand.

'I am sorry.'

The nurse on duty forbade her to speak, and in any case Tushita did not have the strength to say anything else. She glanced towards Shibani who had controlled her tears until then, but as soon as their eyes met, she couldn't stop weeping.

'I love you. First our parents, and now I almost lost you,' Shibani said, kissing her forehead.

'Vivaan . . . please don't tell him anything. I am not asking for much. I promise that I won't ever talk to Andy again. But please don't say anything to Vivaan. Nothing about my condition,' Tushita muttered.

Geet looked towards Shibani, who nodded in agreement. Later, Shibani wanted to tell the police the truth during the inquiry, but Tushita begged her not to. Tushita didn't want any more complications in her life, and for her sake, Shibani remained silent. She had even planned to give Andy a taste of his own medicine by going after him, but Tushita put her foot down there, too.

Slowly, after some days, Tushita started recovering. She couldn't believe she had survived the worst. She thanked god for her new life, and despite the manager's repetitive requests to go back to Kolkata, she decided to continue to live there and manage things on her own. She didn't want to be a burden on any one. She felt guilty for not having listened to her sister and her friends. She told the manager that he should leave once she was discharged from the hospital. He was worried that her condition was critical and she may need support, but Tushita had Shibani, and she was all the support she would ever need. Meanwhile, Vivaan tried to contact the girls, but none of them seemed available. Andy had no clue either, when Vivaan asked him. Though worried, he had no option but to wait. Tushita was heartbroken but pretended to be strong just for Shibani and Geet. A girl's heart is a fragile thing. Break it once and it's never the same.

A week passed by and Tushita was finally out of the hospital. She needed no medicines apart from painkillers. And physiotherapy to strengthen her legs. After settling all the bills, the manager went back to Kolkata. The trio was back in the hostel. Earlier in the week, Geet had informed Vivaan, who was worried about their long absence from college, that they were caught up in some personal work and would return in a few days. Everyone's life had changed forever in a split second.

Geet felt lost in college. Wherever she turned, she saw places where the three of them had spent fun moments. Unlike before, the popular girls didn't humiliate her any more, but she felt lonely. Shibani was at home taking care of Tushita and had informed the professors of their absence.

Sitting in the canteen alone, Geet's mind drifted to the plight of her friend again, so she decided to send her a message. She began typing it on her phone's notepad:

I know that the last few days have been hard for all of us. I do not want you to worry about this because I am pretty sure you will be better soon, and we will be able to do all of the things we did before together. Ever since we met, we have been close. We are each other's soulmates. We have always been there for each other, listening, advising, guiding. You know everything about me—my past, my hopes, my dreams. Likewise, I know everything about you. Many a time, I was a shoulder for you to cry on. You listened to me when I needed you. We became closer while discussing our problems. We both needed a connection—the need to be loved. I always feel that you are the only one who accepts me the way I am and so I can be true to you. You don't expect me to change the way others do. We both are so different but we understand each other so well. I hope our friendship remains this way forever . . . I just hope that you return to college soon, overcoming all the hurdles. Your pain is unbearable for us, and we just want you to live a normal life once again. It is important to mention that your health also depends on the strength you have within you to heal yourself, and I am certain that you will be able to find that strength within you. We will face this difficult situation together and we will be triumphant because life is beautiful and it was made to be enjoyed. Moreover, we have a lot of things left to do together.

She copied the text from her notepad and opened her WhatsApp. Just as she was about to send the message to Tushita, she received a WhatsApp message from Vivaan and, instead of sending the message to Tushita's chat box, she sent the entire message to Vivaan—who was completely unaware of Tushita's health issues until now.

Fuck! Fuck! Fuck! That was all Geet could think of after the huge blunder. She prayed that her 3G connection would not work or her phone would hang, but behind every messed up life, there is a Smartphone laughing at you.

As soon as Vivaan read the message, he called Geet to ask her where she was. The next moment, he was standing in front of her. He had sensed something was wrong but had not expected it to be so bad. And he didn't even know the whole story yet. Once he met Geet, he lectured Geet for lying to him for so many days.

'What do you girls think of yourself? I was so worried, and you didn't even bother to tell me anything. And you call me a friend? Simply wonderful!' Vivaan said sarcastically.

'Vivaan—'

'Now give me some lame excuse and try to defend yourself and your friends. One thing is proved by all this—I am a moron. A big moron who cares for you and treats you like family. Family, my foot!' Vivaan was so angry that his hands were shaking.

But Vivaan was also really scared. He wanted to know what exactly had happened to Tushita. Geet had no choice but to narrate the entire story to him, and tried to convince him that Tushita had instructed them not to tell him. Vivaan was shattered. He could not imagine that Andy would do something like this. He could not bear to think about the pain Tushita was going through.

'Trust me, I am not lying. Tushita didn't want to bother you. Shibani blamed you partly for this accident because you are Andy's friend.' Geet said, feeling helpless.

Without a word, he began walking to the girls' hostel. He was aware that he was breaking the rules but he didn't care about them at the moment. He went to the warden and sought permission to see Tushita. The warden saw the look on his face and bent the rules. With heavy legs, Vivaan walked through the corridor and reached her room. As he knocked, his heartbeat increased as he was about to see Tushita for the first time after her accident. Shibani opened the door.

'Please go away. There is no need to show any sympathy. Thank your friend for us and also tell him that I am quiet only because of my sister.' Shibani spoke to him in a menacing tone through gritted teeth.

'Di, please. Let me meet Tushita. I could never have imagined Andy was capable of something like this. I rarely talk to him these days.' Vivaan tried to convince Shibani.

'I have never liked you from the day I met you. Now I don't ever want to see your face. Just get lost from here.'

'But what have I done? I am worried about her. Please let me see her. Let me come inside. Where is Tushita?'

Shibani was boiling with rage. She thought that a friend of Andy's could not be very different from Andy. All men were the same to her and Vivaan was no exception. She was about to shut the door but she heard Tushita calling out to him. Shibani turned towards Tushita, who was resting in bed, and gave her an angry look. Tushita's expression melted Shibani and, against her better judgement, she stepped aside to let Vivaan enter.

'Did you meet your best friend this week or is he busy harassing some other girl?' Shibani could not help herself.

'Di, please. Vivaan is not that close to Andy. When will you understand?' Tushita said, raising her voice.

'Yes, you are right. In fact, *I* am close to Andy. *We* are *chaddi* buddies,' Shibani said and put on her leather jacket as if preparing to leave.

Vivaan didn't utter a word. He was not in a state to argue. He just kept staring at Tushita as she tried to hide her pain with a smile. No one spoke for the next few minutes. Shibani slammed the door shut behind her as she left the room. Silence filled the air—an awkward silence. Vivaan could see Tushita's eyes fill with apology while she could see his eyes fill with concern. When a person can see the pain behind your smile, words behind your silence, and love behind your anger, you can be sure that you have found your best friend.

Tushita was about to say something when Vivaan interrupted, holding her hand, 'Let's go for a walk. Can you walk? I can't see you like this on the bed.'

'Doctors have strictly recommended bed rest,' Tushita said, avoiding eye contact.

'To hell with them. Nothing will happen. Come on, get up. I am there with you, don't worry. I will hold you if you feel weak . . .' Vivaan stood up.

'I don't feel like it,' Tushita muttered.

'What?'

'I mean, I am not feeling good at all. I am hungry,' Tushita revised her statement.

Vivaan just smiled and took out a sandwich from his messenger bag. Vivaan saw her struggling to use her injured hand, so he picked up a piece from the plate and fed her. Tushita loved the care and attention, and thought of how different two people could be. On the one hand was Andy, who never cared for her this way, and on the other hand, there was Vivaan, who seemed to know exactly what to do to make her feel better.

She kept glancing at him all the while as she ate the sandwich. Friendship is not about rules you set for each other. It's about love, commitment, respect, trust, and the fact that you do not give up on the other. For the next couple of hours, Vivaan made her smile, laugh and forget her pain completely by regaling her with pranks being played at college on unsuspecting professors. Though she didn't move from her bed, Vivaan made her world go round with his gesture. Was she falling for him? Or was this what people called being on the rebound? It was certainly something more than friendship for her. Undivided attention and unconditional love are the two precious gifts that a girl expects from her guy. Vivaan was certainly giving her both, expecting nothing in return. As soon as Vivaan left, she opened her diary to pen down her thoughts:

> *Tushita's prince, who lived in her dreams, seemed to come out of the fog finally, walking towards her. His face was still blurred but her thoughts were now crystal clear. She had always been confronted by this question. Did she really need to save him in some protected, hidden folder? He was a nice guy, respected women, had a sound head on his shoulders, supported her dreams and looked nice enough. There was nothing wrong in considering him her prince. Each day, she would be thankful for spending time with him and would get to know who he really was, what his dreams and secrets are. The tenderness of his heart and the sweetness of his soul captivated her, and left her feeling fortunate. His masculinity made her feel safe and left her longing to be engulfed in his arms. But would Tushita's prince accept her the way she was? She was currently heartbroken and emotionally shattered. However, Tushita believed that her prince would pamper her like never before. To her, being everything to someone was more important than being something to everyone.*

Thug Life: My Popular Fake Boyfriend

Geet's mornings were almost like clockwork. She would help Tushita and Shibani with breakfast and then head to college. She did the same that day, and as she entered the college gate, she felt all eyes on her. Everyone seemed to be laughing at her. She couldn't understand what was going on. Her heart skipped a beat at the thought of the truth being exposed.

No, this can't happen at this time—when I am alone. Is my Fate so fucked up?

Without talking to anyone, she rushed into the washroom and was shocked to see the walls. Graffiti screamed gossip about her:

Faking the loss of virginity
Sleepless, memorable nights of Geet
Blowjob queen Geet

She couldn't believe her eyes. She had no clue how it had happened, but never in her scariest nightmare had she expected the truth to come out in this manner. Just as she was coping with the agony of the last few days, another heartbreaking chapter had begun to unfold. With tears in her eyes, she went to the canteen to confront the popular gang, but she was extremely disheartened when she saw similar messages on the walls of the canteen. She couldn't face the humiliation any more and broke down completely.

'Show us the photograph of your boyfriend, or some proof that you have lost your virginity. Prove your fake boyfriend was real, you slut,' one of the girls from the popular gang ordered.

'You think you are cool by defaming me like this?' Geet sobbed.

'To hell with your fame. Show us proof or make your peace with this.'

'I don't need to prove anything. If you think that I lied about having a boyfriend, then so be it. You have always tried to pull me down and hurt me with your words and actions. I digested every hurtful word, but I am human, too, and there is a limit to how much torture one can bear. It hurts. I just hope god never puts you in such a humiliating situation ever.'

Geet was deeply hurt by the public shaming and started to walk towards the gate when suddenly the peon came to inform her that the principal had summoned her immediately.

'Now? But why? I didn't do . . . anything,' she fumbled.

'I don't know, madam. I am just informing you,' the peon said.

'Is he going to expel me from the college? My career will . . .' Geet could hardly speak.

The peon accompanied her to the principal's cabin and asked her to wait outside. She had goosebumps thinking about the consequences she may have to face. The door to the cabin was slightly open and she stood outside waiting for her turn. She peeped in and the principal was shouting at Rudra for his low grades and warning him that if he didn't score enough marks in the next semester, he would not be considered for any extracurricular activities. He added that Rudra would need to call his parents if he continued to show negligence towards academics.

Geet stood outside silently looking down at her feet thinking about all the possible outcomes of the meeting. The door flew open and she locked eyes with Rudra for a few seconds before he walked away. Geet turned to look at him as he walked down the staircase, when she heard the principal calling her name. Immediately, she went inside the cabin.

'Have a seat,' the principal said in a heavy tone.

He offered her a glass of water, while sipping from another glass. She declined it even though her throat was dry with fear. Somehow she managed to make eye contact with the principal, and before he could say anything she began apologizing, 'I am sorry, sir. I have no clue who did all this but I swear I am not involved in such things.'

'I thought you are a brilliant student and wouldn't fall for this kind of nonsense. Was it my misconception?'

Geet was always a topper and the principal was aware of it.

'This won't be repeated. Please forgive me this time.'

The principal decided to let her go after a stern warning. He did not want to expel her, since her past record was good. Geet just wanted to feel normal again and was tired of whatever was happening in her life.

Why did I live a lie for short-term gains? Geet started walking towards the canteen. Though the principal had assured her he'd find the minds behind this prank, she knew somewhere that the girls were smart enough not to leave any proof behind.

She allowed people to take advantage of her silence. Her life had come crashing down because of one lie. She felt depressed. She didn't have the strength to deal with the humiliation and deep down she knew it was her fault, but at this moment there was no one she could talk to.

As she reached the canteen, everyone was waiting to insult her further. She tried to avoid paying any heed to the sarcastic comments and taunts, and was trying to escape from this hell. That's when Vivaan entered the canteen and shouted out, 'Geet . . . Geet . . .'

She knew he would have nothing new to say to her. She was tired of hearing the same thing over and over again. She had guessed that by now Shibani and Tushita must have heard about it, too. She wasn't wrong. When she checked WhatsApp, there was a message from Shibani: *I know everything. Though there was no need to lie about such a small thing, there is no need to get upset either. I am coming right after giving food and medicines to Tushita. See you in college.*

'Geet . . .'

Vivaan called out once again. She heard him, but sat down at a table with her head hung in shame. Vivaan patted her back and made her stand up and looked straight into her eyes. Geet was unable to respond due to guilt.

'Just look into my eyes . . .' Vivaan whispered.

Geet looked up but all she could see were the faces of those who were openly mocking her.

'Just look here,' Vivaan whispered once more.

Before Geet could understand what was happening, Vivaan leaned forward and kissed her. Geet had her eyes wide open in shock as this had come from nowhere. She couldn't even blink.

'Kiss me back,' Vivaan muttered somehow while still kissing her.

Awkwardly, she kissed him back for a split second, before she withdrew from his embrace. They both just looked at each other, and there was silence in the canteen as everyone watched them. Not a muscle moved.

'That's what I wanted to show these guys . . . now look at their faces. They won't ever question your credibility.'

Vivaan leaned forward once again and this time Geet responded with equal intensity. She closed her eyes in anticipation and her breathing escalated out of both fear and excitement. All the students in the canteen observed every expression that flickered in their eyes. Luckily, everybody was in a state of shock and none of them clicked photographs. When they finally walked outside like a king and a queen, the expression on the faces of those watching were priceless. Even the girls who tried to defame her had their jaws dropped in shock. Vivaan glanced at Geet, who was already looking at him, showing no signs of regret. Within minutes, she had regained her lost respect and shut forever the mouths of those who had questioned her.

'I'm so sorry if that caught you off guard. I hope you didn't mind it. It was just one friend helping out another.'

'Not at all. But how did you know about it?' Geet asked curiously.

'One of my friends told me the entire story and I came running to college. The only way to seal their lips was to seal your mouth with mine. And so I did just that.'

'You should have seen their faces. Oh god, they were so shocked! I just loved it! Thank you so much for being there, but being there always in the same way is not acceptable.' Geet laughed.

'Of course. I just thought that the only way to make this work was to make the fake story real in front of them.'

'And it worked!' Geet added.

Geet and Vivaan continued to talk for some time. Geet also messaged Shibani, telling her that she was headed back to the hostel. Though lying about a relationship was not right, it felt so right to see the shocked expressions on the faces of all those mean collegemates who had been giving her a hard time through the year. Their criteria for being cool and acceptable was to lose one's virginity—how shallow were they? Geet didn't doubt Vivaan even once when he revealed his intentions. Having a friend you can trust blindly was a blessing indeed!

'Had you lost your mind, Geet? How could you be so immature in handling such situations? What did you get by lying about a boyfriend? You could have told me once and I would have sorted this out.' Shibani was boiling with rage.

'At that time, I didn't think of the consequences. I know that it was not right but it's sorted now. 'Geet said politely.

'Geet, you should have at least told us when you got to know today that your secret was out,' Tushita complained.

'It's okay, guys, now just chill. It's all over.' Geet tried to calm both the girls down.

'So, whenever you want to do something like that again, don't worry. I can act as your lesbian girlfriend next time so no dickhead troubles you,' Shibani said jokingly.

Everyone exchanged big smiles and gave each other a hug. More than angry, both sisters seemed upset that Geet didn't confide in them earlier. When Shibani left, Geet narrated the entire Vivaan episode to Tushita. She hadn't brought it up earlier because she knew that Shibani did not like talking about Vivaan. Now seeing Tushita in this state made her even angrier at Vivaan. At first, Tushita was taken aback when she heard that Geet and Vivaan kissed each other, but when she got to know the entire story she was pacified.

'Are you sure you have not started liking him?' Tushita asked teasingly.

'Oh! Shut up. We are just friends. If there was something like this, I would have told you first. After all, I got to know him through you,' Geet explained.

Geet sat beside Tushita and gave her the prescribed afternoon medicines. It is often said that girls can only be enemies, but the fact is, when they become friends, the bond is as strong as one shared by sisters.

The best feeling in the world is knowing that your friends love you just the way you are and wouldn't change anything about you. Geet was lucky enough to have friends who stood by her whenever she needed them. She was just thinking about their first meeting in college and how quickly they had become the best of friends. She was sitting in the library, finally close to finishing *To Kill a Mockingbird*. She saw Rudra walking towards her. She hoped he wasn't coming there to meet her. She kept her fingers crossed, pretending to read the book, but could see him moving towards the table in the periphery. She wanted to bang her head somewhere and tell him that Shibani was not interested in him so that he would stop harassing her.

'Hi Geet!'

She pretended not to hear him. He took the book from her hands. Geet looked up, about to protest when he spoke again. 'Do you want to be my girlfriend?' Rudra asked.

Her eyes widened. She was in disbelief. Did Rudra just ask her out? The person who always asked about Shibani was asking her out. She was not special. At least that's what she felt about herself, and Rudra was the most popular guy in the college!

Why me? I am a nerd. No guy wants to be seen with me. No one even likes me. So why does he want me all of a sudden?

'Why?' she asked him simply.

'Yes. Why you? Why would someone like me go out with someone like you? It just doesn't make sense.'

'I don't know,' Geet said, annoyed at him for putting it so bluntly.

'Well, I know exactly why,' he exclaimed. 'We both need this, to help each other.'

'How would this help us?' Geet said, scratching her head.

'I am weak in studies and my grades are falling. I have to score high in the next semester.'

'And you want to study with me?'

'Actually no, but I think you are the only one who would be up for it.'

'Why do you think I would help you?' Geet was curious to know what he wanted.

'You are not popular, and I know Vivaan is not your boyfriend. So, with me as your boyfriend, you will be popular and no one would ever speak a word about you,' he justified, making awkward gestures.

'Sorry, but I am perfectly happy about my social status,' Geet lied.

'Don't hide it. I know you're not. I have seen people making fun of you. I can make all that go away.'

Geet imagined her life in college if she had Rudra as her boyfriend. She would be the queen bee. Then she wondered why she would *want* to be one of those popular people who had always made her feel worthless.

'No one would believe it anyway,' Geet declared.

'We could make them believe.'

'How?' she asked confused.

'Just like this,' he said leaning forward.

'Umm, no! I don't think I am up for it.' Geet got up from the chair and started walking away.

'Why not?'

'Simply because I am not comfortable with it. Excuse me,' Geet said and left the library.

'No wonder people call you a loser,' Rudra mumbled.

She was not convinced at all. Nobody would believe it and she didn't want any more complications in her life. As she was walking down the corridor, one of the girls tripped her and she fell flat on her face.

'Oops,' the girl said in mock horror.

Geet got up and started to wipe the dirt off her face.

'Don't rub it off. It makes you look better,' the girl said sarcastically.

Geet simply walked away with thoughts that haunted her mind.

Every. Single. Time. They are rude to me without exception. They hurt me physically and mentally, and now I am done with it. I am done with those bullying bitches that make my life a living hell.

She knew only one way to fix this. She just couldn't take it any more. Each person has a threshold that once crossed leads to the person simply losing all calm. She walked back to Rudra who was sitting with his friends. She looked him dead in the eye as she uttered the words.

'Deal.'

He knew exactly what she meant. A sly smile broke on his face. Everyone looked confused, but they both knew what exactly was going on. They were now in a fake relationship, helping each other get what they needed. Geet was Rudra's fake girlfriend and he was her fake boyfriend!

You Need a Makeover, Not a Hangover!

'So, how are we supposed to make people believe that we are suddenly together?' Geet asked.

'Simply by acting like a couple. It shouldn't be difficult,' Rudra added, sipping coffee.

'Yes, but you are missing something major here. Vivaan kissed me in front of everyone a few days ago, and they don't expect girls like me to switch boyfriends this often.'

'No one will think so much. People will think you are just one of those girls I wander about with.'

'What do you mean?'

'You know, I have bets with my friends who challenge me to have sex with them . . . so not girlfriend material but conquests.'

'Does it ever work?' Geet was disgusted.

He gave her a sly smile and laughed. Geet considered that as a yes. She suggested that, since they were planning to act like a couple, it was only fair that they got to know more about each other, but Rudra hardly knew the people he went out with. Those girls were a different deal, and this arrangement was completely new. It was going to last longer than his usual hook-ups.

'Why do people joke about you so much?'

'I don't know. Maybe because of how I dress, or maybe because I am smart. It just makes people dislike me. I am more mature but not good-looking.'

'Maybe you should be a bit more confident,' Rudra suggested.

'I doubt that will work. They will still treat me like shit.' Geet looked sad.

'Well, you are my fake girlfriend,' he said and smiled.

Rudra had a perfect smile, and when he did, his eyes sparkled and his dimples made her melt. His perfectly shaped body was another reason he was so popular. Anyone could see the difference between him and Geet. He was hot while Geet was not. He was charismatic while Geet was awkward at best. He had a large group of friends while she had only three.

'If you want to be popular, you have to change your image,' Rudra said.

Geet knew this but had no idea how to proceed. Rudra checked her out from top to bottom and then advised,

'Well, to begin with, wear some make-up, possibly have your hair straightened. Last, but not the least, get rid of all your clothes.'

Geet nodded. It was not so easy for her to change everything about her all of a sudden. She wasn't comfortable but she thought of giving it a try. There was no harm in pampering yourself. As she reached her room, she thought of taking a shower. She looked in the mirror and started pouting on seeing her reflection, and played with her long hair.

> *Should I change my appearance? No, my make-up does not define me as a person. With or without make-up, I will still be the same person. Yet, I need to make this deal appear believable. Unless I make these cosmetic changes, they will never swallow the fact that Rudra and I are dating. Maybe, I can wear a little make-up, not too much, but just something that looks natural to brighten myself up.*

Tushita was sleeping and Shibani was not in the room. Geet freshened up and thought of using Tushita's make-up kit. She walked to her dresser where the make-up was kept and began exploring. She had no idea what she was looking for. Eyeshadow, lipstick, blush, eye liner—everything was in it. She had never used any of it before and didn't know how to apply them. Instead of messing things up, she decided to take Rudra's help.

'Do you think you could take me to a salon that will help me with my make-up?' Geet asked on the phone.

Her cheeks were flushed. She felt like a teenager asking for her first bra.

'Come on, let's make you more beautiful.' Rudra hung up and texted the name of the salon where he would be waiting for her.

Geet and Rudra exchanged smiles as they entered the salon. Rudra knew a girl who worked there as he had hooked up with her, too, for a week. When he told Geet about it, she just gave him a disgusted look. Rudra defended himself by saying that his hook-up would now help her with her makeover. As the beautician prepared Geet for the hair-straightening process, she glanced at Rudra through the mirror. He motioned her to relax. Gradually, as the process started, she felt calm.

Later, foundation was lightly brushed over her face, and then, to brighten her cheeks, a light pink shade of blush was put on, followed by eyeshadow. That was topped with a liquid eyeliner and mascara on her eyelashes.

'Here is a little lip gloss to make your lips look soft and to give you a stylish look,' the beautician gave her a final tip as she finished her make-up with a flourish.

Geet stood in front of the mirror and looked at her reflection. It was better than she thought it would be. She had a shy smile on her face. Rudra took her to a shopping mall and bought her one of the sexiest outfits there along with a pair of heels. As she tried it in the fitting room, she looked different. She was very pleased with her appearance. No one would believe it was Geet beneath these new hip clothes and make-up.

'One, two, one, two,' she counted in her head as she came out of the trial room, trying not to trip on her heels. As she walked towards Rudra, she was excited. She was scared. She was thrilled. Most of all, she was grateful to Rudra who had made it possible. She had just the right amount of make-up on. Her clothes were elegant and trendy. Rudra was speechless when he looked at her. He was completely mesmerized.

'Wow! You look gorgeous!' Rudra was grinning.

Geet blushed and thanked him for the compliment. As Rudra checked her out, he was full of disbelief. He had never imagined that she could look this beautiful.

'Let's buy a new handbag for you,' Rudra said, now quite excited about transforming Geet's image entirely.

'There's no need for that.'

'Of course there is. The brand of the handbag that your girlfriend uses speaks of your class.' Rudra smirked.

Geet felt pampered. She was getting all the attention she had craved for, even if it was just a fake relationship.

She realized that just because she had pampered herself a little, it did not mean that she had changed herself for someone. It was important to love oneself and Geet had begun to love herself. When she reached the hostel, Shibani and Tushita were surprised to see the change in her.

'Why are you wearing a dress and make-up? Are you unwell?' Shibani asked, touching Geet's forehead playfully to see if she was running a fever.

'I am fine and there is no harm in changing your style a bit,' Geet said, brushing Shibani's hand off her face.

'Changing your clothes is one thing. This is a complete makeover—a Miley Cyrus change.' Tushita laughed.

'Well, do you hate it?' Geet asked worriedly.

'If you like it, we like it. Just a little tip. Work on the blush,' Tushita added with a smile.

'We were just pulling your leg. The truth is that you are looking stunning.' Shibani winked.

Geet looked into the mirror once again as she still could not believe that she was looking good. From her hair to the blush, from her clothes to her heels, she observed what exactly had changed in her. That's when she realized that the real change was not in her looks but in her confidence and in the way she felt about herself. She had started loving herself instead of worrying about other people loving her. We spend so much time investing in money, career and other needs that we forget that real happiness is in investing in ourselves first.

The next day, Geet went to college alone. She took her seat at the back and waited patiently for the class to begin. As she was going through her notes, she was interrupted by two fingers pushing her chin up, and then soft lips touching her cheek. She immediately wiped the kiss from her cheek like a small kid would. She knew it had to be Rudra.

'You are looking great. Just play your part,' he whispered and sat down next to her.

'Well, it looks like the geek actually decided to dress up today. Sorry, but if you're trying to impress someone, dressing nice won't take you far,' a girl from the popular gang hissed.

Geet didn't answer and tried to concentrate on what the professor was teaching.

'I am talking to you, bitch,' the girl said, pulling her shoulders and turning Geet around.

'Please leave me alone,' Geet mumbled.

'What did you say?' she taunted.

Rudra sat silently and nodded at Geet. She took a deep breath and closed her eyes, trying to dig down deep to find her voice. She tried to use the confidence she had recently discovered.

One more deep breath, and she opened her eyes, tilting her head back and looking straight into the taunting girl's eyes. 'I said please leave me alone,' Geet said in a commanding voice.

Their entire popular group started to laugh in their annoying high-pitched voice. They were, however, silenced by the professor. The act continued outside the class once Geet was alone.

'Is something wrong, lovely ladies?' Rudra asked, as he came outside to join them.

'Just this nobody is trying to be somebody,' the girl smirked.

'She can be anyone she wants to be,' Rudra disagreed.

'Oh, is that so?'

'Yup! I know how to treat a person right.'

Rudra took Geet's hand in his and walked towards the parking lot. They didn't speak a word until Geet broke the silence, 'Thanks for sticking up for me. I didn't think you cared that much.'

'I care a lot more than you think.'

'You actually care for me?' Geet questioned.

Rudra held her hand and said, 'I have seen you around campus for quite some time, getting bullied by that gang, but I never did anything. Today when I saw her doing that to you, it made me mad. I do care. I never thought I would care about you but I do. Your help in my studies and your change in appearance are really admirable.' Rudra smiled.

Rudra dropped Geet at the hostel and left. Geet loved the attention she was getting. She had always wanted someone to pamper her, care for her and cherish her. Someone who would look out for her and guard her. The deal was worth a million dollars for her, and her fake boyfriend was playing it well. They might not get a happy ending but it would still be an experience to cherish.

'You have been missing a lot of lectures, Shibani. I think you should start attending a few now,' Geet expressed her concern.

'I will manage. Nothing is more important than my sister. I just want her to get well soon.'

Shibani looked at Tushita, who was busy with her phone. After a few minutes, she looked up from her phone at Shibani and signalled her to ask Geet what had been on both their minds for quite a while. When Shibani didn't ask, Tushita decided to break the silence. 'Are you seriously in a relationship? You are just giving us one shock after the other.'

'What?'

'I heard on the grapevine that you and Rudra are dating.'

'I think, more than lectures, I am missing all the entertainment that's happening around you in college these days. First, the washroom scene, then the kissing episode and now the entire Rudra chapter. Are you okay?' Shibani shot off a volley of questions.

'Chill guys. We are not dating. It's just a deal,' Geet said sipping water from the glass kept beside her.

'Deal? What kind of—'.

Before Geet could answer, her phone beeped with a message from Vivaan:

Stay away from Rudra. He is not the kind of guy you should roam around with. He is a player and I know all his stories. He is just playing around with you for some personal benefit. Otherwise he wouldn't have given a damn.

Vivaan was not wrong but Geet knew that already. She too was using Rudra and it was a win-win situation for both of them. Geet kept her phone aside and disclosed the entire secret to Shibani and Tushita. Initially, Tushita and Shibani were not too happy, but looking at the positive change in her behaviour and overall outlook, they calmed down. They had never heard her speak positively about college, and the confidence was also visible in her body language. Nonetheless, they were concerned about her and were worried about her getting hurt in the future. So they had a long chat and expressed their anxiety about her well-being.

'This is just a mutually convenient arrangement. I was going to tell you, but I wanted to see the look on your faces after my transformation,' Geet clarified.

'Just don't get into it too seriously. Be a little cautious. If you are happy, then we have no issues. We just want you to smile always. Don't get into the bad books of the professors and ruin your grades,' Tushita warned her.

Geet held her hand and promised that she wouldn't let her grades get affected, and neither their friendship. She convinced them that they both meant a lot to her and she would never make them regret being friends with her. All three of them hugged before Geet and Shibani left for college. Friends who are loyal are always there to make you laugh when you are down; they are not afraid to help you avoid mistakes and they look out for you. This kind can be hard to find, but they offer a friendship that will last a lifetime.

Vivaan entered the hostel as soon as Shibani and Geet left the premises. He didn't have to enter secretly now as the warden had given him special permission to meet Tushita once or twice a week. He avoided coming in the presence of Shibani. Tushita loved the way Vivaan pampered her, which had made her fall for Vivaan gradually.

'I am hungry,' Tushita said, resting on the bed.

'Why don't you get up and make something for both of us?' Vivaan said, rubbing his hands in excitement.

'How about other way round?'

'You mean . . .'

'Yes. It would be so romantic. It's really adorable when a guy cooks.'

Vivaan hesitated at first but then decided to make Maggi for both of them. Though he was a good cook and his specialty was chicken, which was not possible at that moment.

'You know why all men should learn cooking like you?' Tushita asked, as he was preparing the noodles.

'I am sure you will tell me even if I am not interested.'

'Ha ha. Yes, of course I will. It's because household help is so expensive these days. So you can practise now before marriage.' Tushita laughed.

Vivaan not only cooked for her but also fed her with his own hands. He wanted Tushita to recover quickly as he found it really hard to see her cooped up in bed day after day. He fed her the last forkful of Maggi when he felt something under him and only then did he realize that he had been sitting on Tushita's leg.

'Oh, fuck! I am so sorry. Shit, I really didn't notice that I was sitting on your leg. You should have told me to move aside. Why didn't you . . . it must be hurting.' Vivaan was apologetic and concerned.

'I can't feel anything below my knees,' Tushita mumbled.

'What?'

'I mean, I didn't realize you were sitting on my legs. The way you were feeding me, I was lost in that. You are really . . . I—'

'Don't be silly, you'd do the same for me. Stop being so formal. Wait, I'll get some water for you.'

Vivaan made her laugh in all ways possible. Then, they watched a movie. Vivaan was the kind of a friend who never expected anything and just selflessly cared for Tushita with no evil intentions. There never was such a friendship that made him feel this way. Tushita had always been there with him when he had needed a friend, and now he was just doing the same for her. Tushita, however, couldn't resist her feelings for him and wanted to express it all but wisely didn't say anything. Once Vivaan left, she just opened her diary and began pouring out her feelings:

Tushita's Prince Charming had absolutely swept her off her feet. How can one be so adorable? Tushita had no words to express. For so long, she had held her heart so securely away from the world, in a cold and dark space. Then he came into her life and she didn't know what to do. She found in him what her heart had so long desired but she was not sure about letting him into her life because of her haunting past. The more time she spent with him, the more intense her feelings became. With each passing day, he impressed her more and more, and filled a space inside her heart that had only known emptiness before. Every time the prince helped Tushita physically, he touched a part of her soul.

Scared of these feelings because they're still new.
She catches herself thinking of the best ways to share,
  hoping he'll reciprocate her feelings and say he cares.
And then she catches herself again . . . and drags her
  thoughts back to reality.
She is back to square one.

Poems are so stupid. She swears she would never do
  this . . .
But this is her PRINCE, and he isn't like anyone she
  has met.

People say dreams have underlying meanings and we
  should not ignore them.
She wants him to know what they mean and wants
  him to hear.
Hear what she is about to say, feel it with her body, see
  it on her face.
Hear it in her words when they converse.
She loves him! She loves him more than she ever
  thought she could!

Flirtationship—More Than Just Friends

'I am going to teach those girls a lesson,' Shibani muttered, looking towards the professor.

'Please don't do anything that will create more trouble in our lives. There is no need for any more impulsive action,' Geet cautioned.

'It is important. I am not going to melt emotionally this time like I did for Tushita,' Shibani added.

Shibani and Geet were attending lectures when their conversation shifted towards the washroom incident. Shibani couldn't accept that her friend Geet had been treated so badly. She decided to take matters into her own hands. After the lecture ended, Shibani excused herself. Geet stayed behind to talk to Rudra. Shibani went outside the classroom and waited for the popular gang to cross the corridor. As soon as the entire group left the corridor, Shibani followed them. As they reached a secluded area in the campus, Shibani looked around to confirm that no one was around. With the coast clear, she quickly walked towards them and grabbed the arms of the girl who was the mastermind of Geet's humiliation.

'You bloody hooker, how dare you pull off such a cheap stunt on my friend? You think you are popular because you are all dolled up? Once your make-up is washed off, no one will even vomit on you,' Shibani yelled.

'Are you her bodyguard? Or a lesbian lover?' one of them taunted.

Shibani swung her hand powerfully and slapped her hard. The impact was such that the girl fell down on the ground. All the other girls were furious but were too scared of Shibani to do anything.

'You are a girl. So act like one, babe,' the girl said, trying to stand up.

'Oh really, I had no idea that my vagina came with a manual. Now I have to learn from people like you? Get lost, or else I will smash your head right away. And don't forget what was told to you. Stay away!'

The girls remained quiet as Shibani walked off from there. She simply couldn't take bullying lightly when it was about her best friend. Tushita had managed to calm her down before, but this time she was indignant. She was strong and always stood up for people who were true to her.

♡

'Shibani . . . let's go.' Geet came running towards her.

'You seem happy,' Shibani commented, as they walked towards her bike.

'Yes. We are going clubbing tonight.'

'We?' Shibani questioned.

'Vivaan is coming along with Rudra and me. I insisted,' Geet said in excitement.

'Oh . . . you mean you are going out with two assholes.' Shibani laughed.

Shibani didn't mean what she said, but she felt insecure about Geet. From the day Geet had changed her attire, there was a change in Shibani's attitude towards her. Even she was unsure why it was happening. While driving, she tried to look at Geet through the rear-view mirror. As they halted at the traffic light, Shibani felt she was making a terrible mistake by looking directly into Geet's eyes; she felt as if she had slipped into some kind of trance. She noticed Geet's eyes looked bewitching and were framed by long dark lashes. Her perfume was intoxicating like never before. Shibani wondered why the perfume made her feel light-headed. Trying to avoid her eyes, Shibani looked down at her lips and noticed how full they were. Shibani shook her head, trying to get these strange thoughts out of her mind and focus on the road. She didn't know what had come over her, whether it was momentary insanity or whether she had smoked too much to think straight. She had been having this strange feeling whenever she was in Geet's company. Was it just because of her hatred for Vivaan or because of Geet's closeness to Rudra? She was anxious but that did not justify her changed behaviour.

'We are on our way. Where have you reached?' Geet asked Rudra while sitting on Vivaan's bike.

'I'm on my way. Will see you directly at LPK,' Rudra said and disconnected.

Geet and Rudra had decided to hang out in Club Love Passion Karma; she had invited Vivaan too. Vivaan was a bit hesitant since he was not sure of Rudra's intentions but he couldn't say no to Geet. Both of them reached the club and were waiting for Rudra. Geet was in love with the architecture and the ambience. She was quite thrilled. Vivaan, on the other hand, was a bit apprehensive because it was an expensive place. Rudra arrived and paid for all three of them. That added to the Vivaan's discomfort, because, though he wanted to pay, he didn't have that much money on him. Geet entered excitedly and was getting herself clicked. Her red dress made her look extremely elegant and Rudra clearly approved.

'You are looking very pretty. I like it.' He winked at her.

'All thanks to you.'

Vivaan walked awkwardly beside them without uttering a word.

'What happened to you, buddy, are you all right?' Rudra tried to strike a conversation with Vivaan.

'Absolutely. Just a little tired,' Vivaan pretended.

As they settled down on the table outside facing the lake, Rudra ordered a hookah. He even got three pints of beer from the bar counter.

'Cheers,' they toasted in unison.

'When was the last time you got completely drunk?' Rudra asked both of them.

Geet just looked at Vivaan and gave a sly smile remembering the warden incident. She narrated the entire episode to Rudra who couldn't control his laughter after hearing Vivaan's strip story. It was bottoms-up for Rudra's drink before he revealed his embarrassing moment: 'The last time we were drunk, we created havoc. We were three friends drunk out of our wits, so we decided to take a cab. The cab driver knew that we were drunk, so he started the engine and turned it off again in a few minutes. He said that we had reached our destination.

The first guy got down and gave him money, while the second one thanked him. I got down from the car and slapped him hard. The driver must have gotten scared that I had understood what had happened. I told him, "Control your speed the next time, you nearly killed us." The next day when we recollected what had happened, we were so embarrassed.'

Geet laughed out loud and almost spilt her drink. Vivaan forced a smile.

'In the act of pretending to be drunk, we girls have done so many dumb things even though we were completely under control.' Geet winked.

Rudra was observing Vivaan all this while and felt there was something he was missing. Rudra sensed that he wasn't too happy about being there but he couldn't figure out the reason behind it. Geet had told him that they were just good friends, and if that was the case, Rudra was a bit surprised by his behaviour. However, he decided to overlook it as they were there to have fun. They all clicked selfies near the lake in different seductive poses. When you are single and out with a couple, your photography skills are generally tested. Vivaan too turned out to be a photographer that night for Geet and Rudra, even though they were not really a couple. After a while, they just stood there enjoying the breeze.

'You want to smoke some weed?' Rudra asked.

'You smoke it daily?' Geet was concerned as Tushita's past flashed in front of her eyes.

'It's been a long time since I smoked.' Rudra was trying to recall the last time he smoked.

Geet relaxed after hearing his answer. Rudra tried to convince her to try it once when the waiter came with the hookah they had ordered. All three of them had finished their drinks by then, so Rudra once again went to the counter.

'Why do you have to try weed? I told you to stay away from him but I don't understand what black magic spell he has cast on you,' Vivaan said angrily after Rudra's exit.

'Vivaan . . . just chill. Did I agree to it? Why are you spoiling your mood? Don't be a spoilsport,' Geet said, inhaling the flavour of the hookah.

'Whatever,' Vivaan said, snatching the hookah pipe from her.

All of them ended up having a ball, with unlimited drinks on their table followed by energetic dancing. Rudra did not know that Geet could dance so well. The DJ blended hip-hop, rock and Bollywood dance numbers perfectly.

'So apart from your brain, your feet too have magic in them,' Rudra said as he held her waist while dancing to a romantic number that was being played.

Vivaan was keenly following Rudra's hand as it slowly moved downwards on Geet's back. He could not bear it any more and wanted to leave the place, so he made up an excuse about his friend not being well.

'I want to dance more. This is not done, Vivaan.' Geet got upset.

'You both can continue. I have my bike,' Vivaan pointed out.

'No, that's fine. We will come again some other time,' Rudra said like a true gentleman, which took Vivaan by surprise. He suggested that Rudra and Geet go by car and he would manage going alone. Rudra offered him a lift but Vivaan chose to go back on his bike. Even the formal hug between them before departing was pretty awkward.

Rudra opened the door for Geet. As he drove, their conversation shifted from one topic to another and eventually landed on Rudra's family. That's when he became emotional. Geet had no idea and regretted bringing it up. 'Well, my dad was not an alcoholic, and I did have him for most of my life, but he left my mom and me for someone else. It was devastating. For about five months, every Saturday, my mom and I would go to the same restaurant he would take us to, and she would just sit there and cry. She could not stop going there because she did not want to let go. She is better now, though I think she still loves him.'

'Do you still love him?' Geet asked.

'I do, but I will never forgive him. You know what I mean?'

'Yeah.' Geet nodded and added, 'Not all marriages end badly.'

'You are right. Not every marriage does, it only happens to people who don't put in the effort to fix it,' Rudra pointed out, touching her face.

Geet looked up at him, into his intoxicating eyes, and then looked down at his lips. He looked adorable and it made her heart flutter and her lips tremble. She saw his dreamy eyes gaze at her and noticed them slowly lower and fix on her lips. Rudra quickly glanced back up. No matter how hard he tried, he couldn't keep his eyes off of her lips. Geet slowly started to glance up and down, eyes to lips, and while doing so, she couldn't help but feel closer to him. Rudra took his time before he reached her lips, and made the final move. They kissed, genuinely and passionately, until Rudra accidentally pressed the horn of his car with his elbow. He pulled back and started driving again without even looking at her. Geet glanced at him a couple of times but Rudra's eyes were locked on the road. There was an awkward silence that filled the air, and Geet just increased the volume of the music to block it out. No one spoke until he dropped her back to the hostel.

'Thanks for the ride,' Geet said, looking at him.

'No problem,' he answered.

'Well, goodnight,' she said awkwardly reaching to unbuckle her seat belt.

'Are we going to talk about what happened?'

'You mean the . . . kiss?'

'It was a little more than just a kiss,' Rudra said.

Rudra was right; it was not just a little kiss, not something she could just shake off. She was in a dilemma as her mind said one thing but her heart said something else. Her heart was beating a million times faster than usual, and all she could do was look at him, hoping that he would want to kiss her again. Her mind kept screaming against it. She could not fall for him. He was a player and was not suitable for her. Moreover, it was nothing new for him. He must have kissed a hundred girls before her and she should probably listen to her mind instead of her heart.

'Maybe we should just forget about it. Let's just stick to our deal.' Her mind won the argument.

'I think that might be the best thing to do,' he agreed slowly, though Geet was hoping he would disagree.

She nodded and started walking towards the hostel gate. Rudra was still waiting. Geet turned back and said, 'By the way, you are taking your father's legacy ahead. You too just roam around with girls and leave them alone without thinking about their feelings, right? As your well-wisher, I hope you won't turn into your father after you get married.' She walked into the hostel.

Rudra stood there motionless. He had never taken relationships seriously. That is what his dad had done too. He had no right to blame his dad since he was no different. In a fraction of a second, Geet had made him rethink his whole life. As Geet went out of sight, he felt a part of him was leaving.

Have you ever held on to the pain for so long that it seemed like you didn't care? When you thought you were crying but when you reached up to wipe your tears, there was nothing there? Just emptiness. Rudra felt something similar as he drove back. He had a smile on his face when he thought about the tender kiss he had just shared with Geet. It was flirtationship. It was more than a friendship but less than a relationship.

Game Over, She Lost!

When you realize you want to spend the rest of your life with somebody, you want the rest of your life to start as soon as possible. Tushita too had realized who that person was for her. Vivaan had come to see her when Geet was about to leave for college. Once Geet left, he was sitting right beside her with the medicines in his hand as she rested on one side of the bed.

'Here's your tablet, madam, get up.'

'I hate medicines and tablets. More than the person who invented math, I want to kill the person who invented such bitter pills,' Tushita said with disgust clearly written on her face.

Vivaan was quite composed and didn't react to her silly comments that continued for a while. He made her sit up straight on the edge of the bed with her legs down while taking the tablets.

Vivaan saw a cockroach sitting on the nape of her neck and told her to sit still. Her T-shirt had a low cut and it exposed more than half her back. Vivaan reached out to catch the cockroach as it started to move under her T-shirt. Tushita could feel the tickling sensation of its movement. As soon as Vivaan touched her back and put his hand inside the T-shirt, she let out a slight moan and closed her eyes. It was a different feeling altogether. After a slight struggle, he caught it and threw it on the floor and crushed it with his feet. Tushita had her eyes shut and could still feel his fingers on her back.

'Wow! You didn't even move an inch. If it was some other girl, she would have turned the house upside down by now,' Vivaan commended.

Tushita had a wide smile on her face not because he appreciated her bravery but because she had loved the feeling of his fingers on her bare back.

Before they could settle down, there was a loud knock on the door. Tushita panicked because she knew it was Shibani. Shibani was the only one who banged on the door instead of knocking. She was horrified by the thought of Shibani seeing Vivaan in her room. She first thought about telling Vivaan to run inside the washroom but then she rejected the idea immediately. 'Come . . . come inside,' Tushita said hysterically.

'Where?' Vivaan said softly so that Shibani wouldn't hear his voice.

Tushita signalled him to hide under the bed so that Shibani wouldn't catch her.

'Are you serious?'

There was no scope of Shibani finding out as Vivaan had hidden himself properly. The door opened and there she was, standing at the door, 'Is Geet not here?' Shibani asked as she slammed the door behind her and went into the washroom.

'She left some time back. Didn't she come to college?'

'Not yet,' Shibani said as she went into the washroom.

'She might be with Rudra then.'

Shibani came out and looked at Tushita carefully. Tushita tried to fake a smile but her hands were shivering. After a few seconds, Shibani started searching for something in her drawer.

'Di, how... how are you early today?' Tushita stammered.

'I am leaving again immediately. I forgot to take my project papers.' Shibani flipped through all the papers in her drawer.

'Got it. I am leaving, do you need something?'

'No, I'm okay.' That was all Tushita could manage.

Shibani opened the door and was about to leave when she turned around and asked, 'Should I keep the wheelchair beside you?'

The moment Shibani uttered those words, Tushita got goosebumps. Her heart skipped a beat in fear and anxiety. Tushita shook her head violently and Shibani left. For a second she thought she would be found out. She hoped that Vivaan hadn't heard it. The secret she had taken care not to reveal could have been discovered. She wanted to run away from reality but couldn't. No one knows how much pain and agony one suffers except the heart of the person who faces it. She didn't want to face Vivaan but she had to tell him to come out from under the bed. The space was so narrow that Vivaan found it difficult to get out. He asked for Tushita's help but she didn't move from the bed.

'You can manage. Push more.'

'I am stuck. What the hell do you mean push more? I am not delivering a baby here.'

Tushita laughed and repeatedly asked him to come out by himself. After a lot of struggle, he managed to do so.

'You could have at least gotten up and pulled me out,' Vivaan complained as he drank the water.

Vivaan sensed that something was amiss. He had been genuinely stuck and had needed help, but Tushita had not even budged. He had also noticed that Tushita had not opened the door and neither had she locked it after Shibani left. What could have been the reason behind that? There had to be some explanation, a bigger picture that he was missing. He was almost sure he had heard a wheelchair being mentioned. He looked suspiciously at Tushita who was smiling as she saw Vivaan looking at her. What was hidden behind that smile, he wondered. Vivaan could see Tushita's expression and thought everything would be all right but he didn't see the dreadful pain in her heart which was so hard to define. He saw her diary on the table and thought of reading it to find the truth behind that sweet smile. He knew that Tushita used to write about her life in the diary, and he sensed that her suffering would be hidden in those pages. With a heavy heart, when Tushita was engrossed in her mobile, he hid the diary inside his T-shirt and pretended to go to the washroom. Keeping his fingers crossed, Vivaan rushed inside and locked the door. He sat on the stool that was kept inside and opened the diary. He tried to console himself that everything would be all right and that it was just his mind playing games with him, but once he started reading, he was lost in it.

Life is hard to live when the light inside no longer shines. Everything around becomes so dark that you think of grabbing a knife to leave a mark just so that you can feel alive again. My fear and doubts are replaced by pain and suffering. I hope to fill the emptiness inside me. I fight to end my loneliness. Failure has consumed my heart, and all of a sudden, my life is not the same any more. My friends care about me but I feel I am a burden to them now. I need support even for the smallest things. What was my fault? Only that I loved someone and trusted him blindly. Now I cannot walk. It is possible that I may never walk again. Doctors say that I need to exercise but I have given up. Every day is a war for me, a struggle to obtain reality. I had a huge collection of footwear but now they're of no use. The pills make me tired but I am left with no choice. I wish I could walk again and live a life which was as normal as before. Now no one will love me, no one will want to marry me. I wanted to be successful but now my future seems bleak. One moment can be so devastating and one action can have such an everlasting impact that it can create permanent scars in your heart. Just a few days ago, I was thinking of living a high-profile life after my education, was hoping to get placed in one of the finest groups of hotels. Today, all I want to do is walk on my own feet. I want to go to the kitchen alone and fetch a glass of water. I want to walk to the window to feel the sunlight on my face. I want to live, I want to smile, I want to laugh, I want to party and I want to go out walking on my own feet, but right now nothing seems possible. My life is suddenly dependent on these two wheels on which my body rests, and my heart cries. Sometimes you don't need someone to pull you out of darkness; you need them to sit there with a candle letting you know you are not alone.

Vivaan was shattered. He just couldn't digest the fact that Tushita could not walk after her accident. He could not understand why she had hidden this from her. He was traumatized by the fact that he hadn't been able to sense her pain for so many days. Why had Geet and Shibani lied? Probably because Tushita had told them to, but why? Teardrops fell down on the page that he was reading. He started flipping through the pages and one of the pages caught his attention.

Tushita met her prince today. He wanted to take her out but she declined. How could she? She was no longer the lively girl who could run everywhere. She had no sensation in her legs and needed a wheelchair for support. Her life was surrounded by people like Shibani and Geet and yet she felt all alone. She is trapped in the wheelchair and her mental agony is unbearable. It's a world where chaos and hatred overtook every bit of happiness that might try to escape. Laughter and smile never seemed to last. Could no one see this smile she was faking, see how, inside, she was constantly shaking? These people all claim they know her well, yet no one can see through her crumbling shell. She whispers that she's fine and they take her word for it. She would hide behind this wall for most of her life—she had managed so far and had dealt with her inner conflicts. Maybe her

acting was convincing enough if no one saw through it. She could fool everyone but not herself. The demons of fear echoed in her head and tormented her all day long, trying to break her. She had once been very strong, but was now growing weak. She could no longer differentiate between reality and fiction because all that she hoped seemed to be an illusion.

'Vivaan . . . are you okay in there?' Tushita called out in concern.

Vivaan managed to reply, 'Coming in a few minutes.'

As Vivaan came to terms with this shocking truth, he felt the life inside him drain away. He turned the page and the diary was blank ahead. He was about to shut it when he saw the last page that read:

Once upon a time there was a girl.
I am happy, she said as she looked in the mirror.
So full of life, full of energy alive.
She knew how she wanted to feel.
She looked around and everywhere she saw love.
She was committed to live her dreams.
Then things changed.
She stopped seeing herself that way.
She let the dark voices come in.

Overwhelmed by the mystery of it all,
the universe turned its back on her.
She could not believe that she had once thought
she was incredibly blessed.
She almost died in desperation and despair.
The determination once so intense began to fade.
Her soul shook
like an ending . . .
Who knows what her fate will be,
Heaven and hell are both a fair game.
Will she succumb to peace or fall down in shame?

When Vivaan didn't come out of the washroom for quite some time, Tushita grew apprehensive. When she had called him a couple of times, his response had seemed normal. When she glanced at the table where she had kept the diary, she found it missing. Her heart started beating a thousand times faster as she understood that Vivaan must have seen it. She had a feeling that he was reading it inside. She panicked at the mere thought of her misery being revealed. Somehow she had managed to hide it from him so far, but the truth would be in front of him now. The only reason she had not told him already was because she didn't want to talk about it. When Vivaan had come to know about her accident, he had rushed to see her. Tushita had, for the first time, felt someone caring for her genuinely, apart from her sister. The affection shown by Vivaan had made her fall for him. Vivaan gave her undivided attention and unconditional love. She was not sure what it was, but it was certainly more than friendship. Her dilemma, however, was whether Vivaan would accept her the way she was now. Luckily, her folding wheel chair was always kept behind the almirah and Vivaan hadn't come to know the full extent of her injuries. Thus she decided to reveal neither her feelings nor her physical condition to him. She even told Geet and Shibani not to reveal anything to Vivaan as she didn't want anyone's sympathy. Shibani was happy not to share anything with Vivaan because, as Andy's friend, she blamed Vivaan equally for the state in which Tushita was now. Geet was initially hesitant about hiding such a big tragedy but Tushita managed to convince her, and after looking at Shibani's anger towards him, she had agreed to keep mum. With every meeting, Tushita's feelings for Vivaan got stronger as he filled a place inside her heart that had known only emptiness before, and by the time she thought of telling him the truth, it was too late. She couldn't gather the courage to speak about it on her own. Suspecting that Vivaan had come to know the truth, she almost suffered a breakdown due to the fear of her hopes of living with him getting smashed immediately. She wanted to walk and speak to Vivaan who was still inside the washroom. She was putting her utmost effort to get up but was not able to manage it. Nevertheless, she continued trying to get up. She pushed herself hard and while her upper body moved, there was no strength in her legs. She fell down on the floor. Helpless and disheartened, she cursed her fate for showing her such a day. With absolutely no energy in the body, tears in her eyes and pain in her heart she tried to crawl ahead putting all the weight on the floor with her hands. After a lot of effort, she could only move a few inches. She wanted to scream in pain but just for the sake of Vivaan, she pushed her body further. However, when she saw the washroom door opening, she gave up.

Vivaan saw her helplessly crying on the floor and immediately rushed to pick her up.

'Why did you have to do that?' Vivaan said as he lifted her up by her shoulders.

Tushita was silent. She just kept looking at Vivaan as he placed her on the bed. There was a haunting silence in the room.

'Where is your wheelchair?' Vivaan asked.

Tushita pointed at the almirah without saying a word. Vivaan took the wheelchair and propped it open near the bed. He made her sit on the wheelchair and looked at her angrily. Tushita kept looking at him as tears rolled down her cheeks.

'Please say something,' she begged.

Vivaan looked up straight in her eyes fiercely and said, 'Thank you for hiding your pain and lying so easily. Thank you for breaking my trust so easily. You are a player, hats off to your acting.'

After saying that, he walked away, slamming the door behind him. Tushita sat there motionless. She gradually moved the wheelchair in front of the mirror and examined herself in disgust, cursing her own life. If she had anything in her hand she would have thrown it with full force at the mirror to express her hatred. She took a deep breath, picked up the diary that Vivaan had kept on the dressing table and started penning down her thoughts:

The prince has departed forever from Tushita's life, leaving behind her tattered dreams of them living together happily. There's a hollow void in the sky tonight. It's swallowing her up, stealing her dreams. Tushita has been missing him and it was evident that this feeling will encompass every piece of her until, by some miracle of god, she is able to forget. Then and only then, piece by piece, she will be whole again. For without him, she is a broken puzzle. People say love lasts forever. These figments of the human imagination are only storybook material. Maybe that is why she lives so often in the world of fiction. It is impossible to get rid of these feelings that weigh down on her like bricks sinking to the ocean's sandy bottom. She sees herself floating in the deep ocean of pain and it is all she can do to prevent drowning. Yet maybe now she could stop trying to stay afloat. Maybe now the right thing to do was let the current of regret and memories wash her away forever.

Tushita was sitting shell-shocked when the realization of Vivaan's anger and departure sank in. A few minutes later, she heard a knock on the door. She moved the wheelchair towards the door and opened it slowly. She thought she was dreaming and pinched herself not once but twice because she just couldn't believe what she was seeing in front of her eyes. Vivaan was standing there with a bunch of flowers in his hands.

'I am sorry for being impulsive. I shouldn't have reacted in such a harsh way,' Vivaan said handing over the flowers to her and shutting the door of the room.

'It's okay. I am sorry for hiding it from you.' Tushita could finally manage a smile on her dejected face.

Vivaan sat near her trying to convince her that the clouds of darkness would pass one day.

'I will do everything I can to spare you pain and preserve your innocence. I won't lie, the upcoming weeks, months or even years may feel like a battle. You will face challenges, but in every challenge, of your life, you will find me standing right beside you. I also promise you today that one day you will once again start walking and will live a life like you did before. You are my friend, and no matter what happens, I won't ever leave you alone in difficult times.'

Tushita hugged Vivaan instantly and felt the warmth of his arms. She was now ready to fight for her life and overcome her fears. No matter how hard we try, there are days when smiles and laughter are nowhere to be found. These are the days when you have to force yourself to feel the opposite of what you are feeling and focus on the little moments of your life. This is the joy you experience in your heart even in the depths of despair and sadness.

Vivaan made her believe that one day she would regain her worth and would no longer feel damaged. She would enjoy desire and intimacy again, and would appreciate the quiet, whispered words of love and ecstatic shouts of passion. With his words, she was geared up to fight with every ounce of her being. Some will touch your heart; some will touch your soul. If you are ever fortunate enough to have someone that touches both, you would be a fool to let them go.

R.I.P. Clothes—Emotions in Motion

'Is it necessary to finish this right now?' Rudra asked Geet as they sat in the library studying for their theory subject.

'Of course. There is no escape from this.' Geet tapped her pen determinedly on the table.

Rudra was not at all interested in studying because he wanted to watch the cricket match that was going on. But Geet was determined to make him understand the topic that day. Once in a while she would look up at his face to make sure he was following the text. It was almost as if she was checking if he was listening at all. She caught him looking at her and she looked right at him and smiled. 'What?'

Rudra shrugged and looked at his sneakers. 'Nothing.'

She closed the book and asked, 'No, seriously, what?'

She knew Rudra was glancing at her occasionally. Deep down, she liked the way he looked at her. His intense looks made her feel weak and she wanted to just surrender herself to him, but her rational mind stopped her every time. Rudra, on the other hand, was getting carried away and had started enjoying Geet's company immensely. He didn't know if this was love, but it was surely different from when he had been with other girls. He just couldn't take his eyes off her.

'I'm just a bit confused. Can you repeat that again?' Rudra came up with an excuse.

Geet repeated and explained it to him once again; he nodded, pretending to have understood it. However, after a few weeks, she could read his facial expressions quite well.

'I know that face. You didn't get it, did you?'

'No.' Rudra bowed his head and looked at his hand.

'Well, in that case, you have some homework.

'But—'

'No buts! You want to clear your exams, don't you? You have two days to revise this entire chapter.'

Geet reprimanded him in a commanding tone and walked towards the music section of the library which was at the far end of the floor. The material there was laid out differently, lying down flat in piles rather than upright, making it much more difficult for anyone to see what others were doing in the adjoining walkway. It was totally secluded. Rudra followed her, and once they were at the end of the walkway, he hugged her from behind. Geet pushed him away instinctively, shocked by his action. This made Rudra lose his balance due to which some music CDs were pushed down. Geet was completely numb and stood as if frozen.

'I think we should put them back,' Rudra said, pointing at the CDs.

'Yes, let's put them back,' Geet muttered, lost.

She was utterly enthralled by him. She would have agreed to literally anything that Rudra would have said at that moment. His grip was firm, yet so gentle. It was like he possessed the power to crush her if he wanted to, but he wouldn't because he didn't want to hurt her. She wanted him to touch her body, to feel her all over, both outside and from within. She was completely spellbound and had her one eye on the walkway in case anyone spotted them. Rudra sensed her apprehension and took a step forward decreasing the gap between them. Geet skipped a heartbeat as he leaned in.

'It's okay,' he said. 'I have been here before, no one ever comes here.'

'Except me,' she said.

'Yes,' he replied, 'and you are already here.'

Geet wondered if he had brought other girls there but soon she let the thought go as Rudra ravaged her lips with his, her body with his hands. His hands were confident and slightly rough but it seemed like he was handling Geet perfectly. She had never been in a situation like this before and it excited her. This was definitely not part of their deal. Knowing that at any moment someone could walk around the corner and catch them made it intensely exciting for her. The moment Rudra realized that the more intimate they got, and the more Geet feared getting caught, he stepped away from her. Geet didn't speak a word and looked towards the walkway and then down at her sandals. Rudra just kissed her cheek and said, 'Let's go. A long ride, maybe?'

Geet just smiled as she had already surrendered herself to him. She had given up all forms of resistance that her mind had applied to her heart. Though he might have had a flamboyant image, there was a certain charm in him that attracted Geet and she was ready to get passionately involved with him.

As they went towards the parking area of the college where Rudra had parked the car, he saw that there was no one there. There was an air of anticipation accompanied by an overwhelming feeling of love. As they both came closer, their excitement was at its peak. It was one of the purest moments when they hugged each other. On the drive to Rudra's apartment, where he lived alone, Geet reached over and rested her head on his shoulder, softly caressing his neck. She then started playing with his hair hinting at what really was on her mind. He stopped the car in a secluded corner in the middle of nowhere. He climbed into the passenger seat and they were so caught up in the act that they didn't even see a tractor speeding towards them across the field until it parked right against the chain-link fence separating them, giving the driver a clear view of their shenanigans. Rudra and Geet awkwardly stumbled out of the passenger side while the driver continued to look at them. No words were exchanged with that curious stranger as they settled back and sped off. When they reached Rudra's apartment, they were still laughing about the driver's shocked expression.

Rudra's apartment was huge though he lived alone. It had all the amenities that one needed for a luxurious life. It was not a rented apartment but a small villa that his dad had bought in Goa during his schooldays. They often stayed there when they visited Goa during vacations, but at the moment it was only Rudra and Geet in the villa with a long cosy night ahead of them.

Rudra took Geet to his special room that was lit up with dim lights and artificial candles. Geet felt so relaxed due to the ambience that the vibes in the room alone were enough to turn her on. The candles were red, pink and white in colour, creating an inviting, sensual atmosphere in the room. The exotic incense sticks acted like a love drug for the two of them. The bed had coffee-stain-coloured satin sheets along with artificial flowers that looked fresh and romantic. As Rudra played a song called 'Let's get it on', he came close to Geet and wrapped his arms around her. Lifting her and gently placing her on the bed, he reached for a 'sex timer' from his drawer which was nothing but a hourglass, with marks at particular intervals suggesting a tag for the person depending upon his stamina. The first tag was 'waste of time' followed by the 'beginner', 'lover', 'playboy', and at the peak was 'sex god'.

'Let's test ourselves today,' Rudra said, showing her the timer and keeping it on the desk beside the table.

'You are such a—'

'Ssssh . . . just stay calm and relax. It's time for you to feel heaven.'

'You had to go to your friend's party, it looks like you have forgotten that,' Geet said, lacing her fingers through his.

'I don't care. All I care about is talking to you,' Rudra added.

Those words made her feel special. She tried not to smile to give away the weakness of her flesh. Rudra started kissing her neck and licking her earlobes. Geet was experiencing this for the first time and the tickling sensation made her go wild. The blood in her veins flowed faster than ever before. Slowly he unbuttoned her top to kiss her belly button. She moved her hips in the air in bliss. Making it slow, he was exploring every inch of her body when he moved downwards to kiss her feet. Slowly he came upwards pulling her skirt up to her waist, exposing her well-toned thighs. Rudra was hard and wanted to rush, but it was their first time and he wanted to make it special. All the clothes were lying on the floor when they stood up and Rudra told her to lie on the mat that he had spread across the bed. He grabbed the massage oil to use on Geet.

'I will be your masseur today.' Rudra winked, pouring the warm oil on her back. 'Is there anywhere you would like me to focus on, Geet?'

'My whole body, please.'

'Okay then, I will make sure I take good care of you and will give you the best massage you have ever had.'

She lay on her stomach with the towel covering her lower half, and he started massaging her shoulders and neck, spreading the oil on her arms and back. He loved her body and he was completely turned on. He was massaging every part of her body. He was no massage therapist but was doing his best to give Geet pleasure by pushing and kneading her muscles. After a few minutes he slowly worked down to her bottom and legs, and removed the towel.

'May I add more pressure, madam, your body is very tense down here?' Rudra acted as if he was a professional.

'Yea . . . yeah do whatever you need to.' Geet was so mesmerized by this sensual experience that she was stuttering as his hands glided down her sides.

He could barely contain himself as he worked his way around her legs and feet but he was still trying to make it memorable for Geet. 'Do you mind if I move a little further down?'

'Mmmmm,' Geet said, but it sounded more like a moan.

Geet was enjoying the sensation as he continued to run his hands between her thighs. Rudra occasionally stroked himself to relieve the tension that was building, hoping she would reach out and take it in her hand any moment. Rudra told her to turn over, tapping her thigh, and she did without covering herself. He got the oil and poured it on her body and just watched as the oil slid down her curves. As Rudra sat there, she was completely relaxed now, soaking wet, and he was bringing her closer to orgasm with every stroke of his finger. Rudra glanced at the hourglass and saw that they had already cleared the 'beginner' tag. Geet bit her lips as she gave him a smile.

'Can I feel you?' Rudra sought permission.

Geet was impressed by his sincerity. 'It's my first time. Please be . . .'

'I will be gentle, baby. Enjoy the ride,' Rudra whispered in her ears giving her a slight peck too.

When Geet reached out for him, he could feel the most intense rush, as if every nerve ending in his body had come to life at the same time. Rudra moaned in pleasure as she continued sliding down in motion.

'Yeah, right there,' he said. 'That feels so good, keep doing that, yeah.'

Rudra returned the favour and Geet was floating in the air with extreme desire and passion.

'Ah, that feels so good, oh god!' She let out a faint and joyful appreciation of their experience.

'People probably remember god more often during sex than at the time of offering prayers,' Rudra said as both of them were stroking each other as they made love.

She moaned in pleasure and whispered softly, 'Why don't we go all the way?'

Rudra was more than ready to do that. He pulled her close to him and positioned himself, pushing with authority, rubbing his fingers on her hips in rhythm with his thrusts.

Geet's voice was now loudly calling out in climax. He slowed down and eventually stopped, holding her tight around the waist, as she let out a long breath. She lay down next to him, out of breath from their passionate lovemaking. Rudra took the hourglass in his hand. The sand had come to settle on the 'lover' tag.

Geet and Rudra did not realize when they had begun to have feelings for each other. Their role play had given birth to a relationship. Geet remembered the first time she talked to him; she wasn't sure what to do as no one used to treat her like a human being before. This was something different, something that led to a new start in her life. Though neither of them had proposed to each other formally or declared the start of a relationship, they felt comfortable in each other's arms.

'Tushita, you cannot just give up like this. Shibani is not wrong when she gets angry with me. I remind her of Andy. You have just given up on your life. Imagine how difficult it will be for her if it is so painful for me to see you like this. It hurts.'

Tushita looked down at the floor.

'Are you not moving because you are in pain or are you in pain because you are not moving?' Vivaan asked. Tushita had no answer to offer.

Vivaan wanted to bring her back to her normal life. When he had asked Geet, she had told him that doctors had advised her to exercise regularly if she ever wanted to get back to normal, but Tushita avoided it since it was such a painful process. However, Vivaan was determined and had brought ankle sand weights for her to exercise. He had made her lie down on her stomach on the bed and had told her to lift her legs slowly. Tushita was not ready to even move her leg an inch but Vivaan carefully held her leg and pushed it upwards.

'Please . . . stop that . . . fuck . . . it hurts . . . Viv . . .' she screamed in pain.

'Push, push . . . don't worry, I am here. Just trust me,' Vivaan said calmly.

'That's it. That's it. I can't do it any more.'

'Please do it for me. Try it once more.' Vivaan looked into her eyes.

That look gave Tushita the strength to conquer the negative forces in her life and to apply strength against her pain. He then made her do several exercises one after another, making her move her legs in all directions, forcing her to fight the odds. He even made her sit at the edge of the bed and pull up her legs, using the strength of her thighs. Once she was able to do it with a little help from him, Vivaan applied the sand weights to her ankle and repeated the exercise. Ideally, he wanted her to do it without weights, but looking at the level of confidence in her eyes, he went ahead and it proved to be fruitful. After an hour of hardcore exercise, Tushita was almost on the verge of collapse but at the same time she also felt confident about herself.

'It's not done yet. I am taking you out around the corridor,' Vivaan said, bringing the wheelchair closer to the bed.

'You can't be serious.' Tushita was shocked.

'Why are you doing all this?'

'I am your friend. Do I need to say more?' Vivaan smiled, and without making too much of the situation, he helped her sit on the chair.

She had that smile on her face that Vivaan was desperate for. He made her laugh, smile and encouraged her to live once again. As they roamed around the corridor, Tushita felt like she was alive after a long time. She felt like she had someone who would never let her die within and would always hold her hand through bad times. Someone who would walk along with her in the journey of life fulfilling her dreams and fantasies. After spending some time out there, Vivaan did something unbelievable. He picked her up in his arms and took her downstairs.

'No . . . someone might come . . . Vivaan, this is risky.'

She kept on protesting but Vivaan paid no attention to her. He kept looking at her until they reached the ground floor. Making her sit carefully on a table there, he went upstairs to bring the wheelchair and took her for a round around the hostel. The warden saw them but had no objection to it when she saw the smile on Tushita's face. No rules and regulations could come in the way of the happiness that reflected in her eyes. Tushita's prince was not a fictitious character who came alive only in those closed pages of a diary but he was in real and had also become the prime reason of her survival.

'Thank you. I guess I needed someone who would help make my life feel normal again.'

'I will fulfil my promise. All I need is a little effort from you. Your smile can do wonders and it should never get lost in the sufferings of the past.' Vivaan kissed her forehead giving her a reason to rejoice.

They both sat on the steps gazing at the sky upwards, wondering about life. Vivaan was thinking about how unfortunate life can be while looking at Tushita's situation; while Tushita was thinking about how fortunate life could be with the right companion next to you.

Tag Me Forever in Your Life

It is amazing how when one person enters your life, you no longer remain the same person you used to be. You might have been careless, arrogant, or someone who never believed in true love. Yet, it takes only person to change these views forever. Geet had unknowingly changed Rudra for the better and had captured his heart permanently. Never in his life had he believed in love but it had all started the day Geet showed him that he was the mirror image of his dad. Rudra was confused about what Geet thought of him. Did she really love him or was it still just a deal for her? He wasn't sure. He decided he needed to find out once and for all. He messaged Geet: *What is our relationship status? I don't understand our relationship. Sometimes, we're friends. Sometimes, we're more than friends.*

Geet was in her room with Shibani and Tushita when she saw an unread text on her mobile. Just one text from Rudra would change her entire mood. She had an instant smile on her face as she anticipated what was going to happen next. Girls are extremely insightful. She too had fallen for him and one can never be 'just friends' with someone you have fallen in love with. Nonetheless, she thought of teasing him.

Geet: *Friend-zoned?*
Rudra: *I thought we are more than just friends.*
Geet: *Yes, you are my fake boyfriend. Forgot?*
Rudra: *Hmmm . . . and in real life?*
Geet: *Not sure. You are a player.*
Rudra: *I am no more. I feel like I should take early retirement after having met you.*
Geet: *I am sure you will still play the IPL. Retired players join that league.*
Rudra: *No one would bid for me in any auction though, once I am with you.*
Geet: *I want you to say it officially.*
Rudra: *How?*
Geet: *My birthday is coming.*
Rudra: *What do you want?*
Geet: *A ring.*
Rudra: *Okay, you will get a ring on your birthday.*

Geet: *Really? Thank you so much.*
Rudra: *Yeah, really, but don't pick the call. I don't have enough talktime left.*
Geet: *WTF. Get lost.*

Rudra was typing for some time and Geet kept starting at the screen. For almost a minute there was no reply but she could still see the typing notification on the chat window. She thought her phone had hung but even after closing down the app and restarting it, the 'typing' status was visible. She wanted to message him again but avoided doing it since she didn't want to appear desperate. She started the long and drawn out cycle of overthinking but fortunately, she finally received a text.

Rudra: *It is evident that you have beauty and charm. No one can deny that. Anyone with the slightest amount of sense in their head can tell that you're magnificently made. I know this better than anyone else, having been given the opportunity to study you so intently all these months but there is far more to you than cute dresses, or even your stunning skin. Geet, it has been the greatest honour to be given the chance to get close to you and look beneath the surface at you as a person.*
Geet: *Awww.*

Rudra: *Everyone may admire you for the things I spoke of a moment ago—your charm, your beauty—but it is for me alone to know you in the most intimate way. That privilege is the greatest gift I have ever been given; you will always be my clearest evidence of divine providence.*
Geet: *Awww.*

Rudra was dreadfully irked because even after sending such long intimate messages, all he got was monosyllabic replies. He wanted to bang his head somewhere but stayed patient until she replied.

Geet: *Will you make it special for me?*
Rudra: *Wait and watch. See you in the afternoon. I will pick you up at 5 p.m.*
Geet: *Need to be back at the hostel latest before 10 p.m.*

Rudra agreed and Geet couldn't suppress a smile when she thought about everything that may be coming her way. She was very excited to start the new chapter of her life that she had never thought would be written. Indeed, the most wonderful feeling in the world is to be loved overwhelmingly by someone you never thought you had a chance with.

Being in love means being yourself. So when you find someone who accepts and appreciates you for who you are, never let them go. Rudra had accepted wholeheartedly that he had fallen madly in love with Geet and he was determined to never let her go. He had booked one of the most exotic places in Goa to make sure that the evening was unforgettable. He had also confirmed with the owner to ensure that all his special requests were implemented at the time of their arrival at the destination. He wore a smart, white T-shirt and a black jacket with distressed blue jeans. Rudra was on his way to pick Geet up from her hostel. As he reached the gate, he saw Geet walking towards him in a dazzling red spaghetti top and denim shorts with high gladiator sandals.

'You have learnt to carry yourself well. I am impressed. Your smile simply adds to your impeccable style,' Rudra said, opening the car door for her.

Geet thanked him with a ravishing smile and took her seat as Rudra cruised towards their destination in Morjim, North Goa.

'So, where are we going? What's the special plan?' Geet asked in excitement.

'Woof Woof.' Rudra winked.

'What's that? Is it some kind of an animal?'

'It's just the beginning, baby. You will see the real Goa today.' Rudra accelerated the car.

Once they reached their spot, he parked the car and the staff escorted them to the Morjim Turtle beach. Geet was thrilled at the thought of Rudra's mysterious plan and was also nervous since no one had ever done anything of that sort for her. Rudra ensured Geet was comfortably seated and disappeared for a couple of minutes to meet the manager. Once everything was set, he took Geet along with him to surprise her with one of the best evenings of her life.

'Can you please give away the suspense now?' Geet couldn't control her anxiety.

'We are going on a private yacht that I have booked for a couple of hours. We will be away from land and its boundaries. It will be the perfect opportunity for us to unwind and enjoy each other as much as we want,' Rudra declared.

Geet was awestruck when she heard what Rudra was saying. She couldn't stop herself from hugging him. Their journey to explore the breathtaking backwaters of the Chapora River in total privacy began on a 50-foot, hand-crafted teakwood boat which was equipped with red and white cushions, curtains and sun beds on the upper deck and one of the best sound systems. It was stocked with a diverse selection of alcohol that ranged from champagne and wine to beer and cocktails. It was accompanied by mouth-watering food that had been carefully selected by

Rudra. He had requested for rose petals to be spread on the deck and all over the floor, which had been done flawlessly by the team.

As they entered the boat, Geet was awestruck by the gorgeous rose petals. She just couldn't take her eyes off the scenic beauty and sunset which she had never seen except in movies. 'Is this for real?' she asked, looking at the birds flying around.

Rudra reached for her from behind and held her in his arms, turning her face to look into her eyes. He made her sit on the couch. A bottle of champagne in an ice bucket was sitting on the table in front with a note attached to it. Geet looked questioningly at Rudra and he motioned for her to read it.

Your smile swallows my heart; it is a perfect punctuation for the only joy I've known to truly be contagious. You effortlessly season all your words with grace but that's because you bring them forth from the overflowing storehouse of love I've seen inside your heart. You're incredibly delicate, you soften my heart with your gentle touch and tender voice. You are also a tremendous source of strength, from where I seek restoration and renewal for my soul. You're my love, my one and only home.

You're the fruit of blessing that I survive on. You're all the places I wish to travel to, and the reason for the rebirth of every dream I had given up on before I met you. You

know I have a lot to learn about life and living but in my 20 years I've learned one important truth: true love is eternal because it proceeds from god. Before meeting you, I never thought it was for real since people like you were never around me. Yet, you made it possible. You made me believe that love exists. I look forward with the greatest faith, hope and love to share an eternity with you.
Yours forever,
Rudra.

The note had a postscript but before reading it, Geet looked at Rudra, who was sitting with two glasses of champagne in his hands waiting to raise a toast to his girl. She looked back into the note and read,

PS: If all this has been too ambiguous and if I've somewhere missed the message I wanted to convey in the midst of the sea of words I have thrown at you, let me simply add: I want to make a home with you, have kids with you and love you no matter what our future holds.

Rudra made her feel like she was the most special person in the world. He made her feel like she was the only star in his sky, lighting up his entire life. Geet was astonished beyond words at Rudra's affectionate revelation. She had to pinch herself to confirm that all this was real. No amount of words could be uttered, no songs could be sung and no gesture could be made to show her love for him, for the love she had for him had no definition. Tears of happiness filled her eyes as she looked at Rudra who bent down to grab the orchids which were kept under the table. Handing over the flowers to her, he said, 'I'm not perfect. I'll annoy you, make you mad, but putting all that aside, you'll never find someone who cares and loves you more than I do. Having you in my life has brought me more happiness than a lifetime could bring. You've touched my life so deeply that now there is no going back. I feel like I was searching for you my entire life. I love you, Geet, and I will love you till my last breath.'

He kissed her cheeks and hands with a promise to be there for her forever. After settling down for a few minutes, Geet broke her silence: 'I was scared to love you at first, out of fear that you would hurt me, but I did it and it's the best thing I've ever done. Everyone told me that you would never understand a girl's feelings but I can proudly say that no one can make a girl feel special like you can. You make me feel safe when I'm near you, lost in your arms. Before I met you, people called me a nerd, made fun of me and humiliated me. Since the day you have come into my life, my heart has gotten a new lease of life. I never thought that within a few days of pretending to like each other, we would be sitting here in the middle of this endless sea and saying these wonderful things to each other. When I found you, a new me was born. You are my everything. Thank you for loving me the way no one has. You understand me and know just how to make things right. You will never know just how much I love you but I will spend the rest of my days trying to show you. You saved me from the worst, and you have been there for me since. No matter what, there will never be another one for me and I will always keep you safe. I love you . . . for all eternity.'

They had together conquered the greatest challenge of life—finding true love.

Rudra and Geet had no similarities, but they fell for each other unexpectedly. As the yacht cruised further and further away from land, they enjoyed the enthralling beauty with the bewitchment of love surrounding them. Each moment together was giving them the greatest pleasures of life and they kissed, exploring each other's tongues passionately, music playing in the background. They danced to the tunes, looking into each other's eyes. As their bodies swirled, their lips were glued together for a long time till Rudra moved back and asked a crew member to bring in the next surprise he had planned. He had arranged for a couple of sky lanterns to the mark of a new beginning of their togetherness.

'I just cannot believe that you can be so romantic,' Geet smiled.

'What did you think? That apart from being good in bed, I was good for nothing?' Rudra smirked.

'Who said that you are good in bed?' Geet teased him as he prepared the sky lantern to launch it in the air.

'Oh yeah? Should I remind you of your wild moans?'

'Shut up,' Geet said, giving him a light peck on his lips.

They both held the lantern vertically and lit the fuel, allowing the hot air from the flame to inflate the lantern. Rudra told her to make a wish quickly.

'I just wish that our smiles will never vanish from our faces, and even if they do, then we will make the effort to put those smiles back on each other's faces.'

'Love you, baby.'

'Your wish?' Geet asked curiously.

'My wish has already been fulfilled. Nothing can be more desirable than to be with you over here. It is my dream, and I am living it,' Rudra said.

After a minute, they felt a gentle upward tug when they let it go. The sky lantern floated up into the night sky, giving out a beautiful warm glow. Geet wrapped herself around him, looking at the lantern as it floated up. As the lantern vanished into the sky, they saw a dolphin jump out of the water twice. Geet jumped on the boat in excitement as she had never experienced a sight like that before. The glitter in her eyes was unbeatable.

'Sir, it's very rare to see a dolphin in the entire trip. It hardly ever happens,' a crew member disclosed.

Sometimes it's the little things that matter the most. Every moment Rudra and Geet spent together was magical. You meet thousands of people and none of them really mean anything to you and then you meet that special someone and your changes forever. The names Rudra and Geet resembled music, but they had never thought that they would mean everything to each other and play the symphony of life together.

Save the 'Date'

There comes a point when you love someone without thinking about whether they are good or bad. You just love them the way they are. Despite having completely contrasting personalities—with no common interests, Rudra and Geet loved each other unconditionally. Geet had never been afraid of loving him but had only been afraid of him leaving her for someone else. She was petrified at the thought that his kisses and smiles were not genuine. Her mind kept reminding her heart that he was the most popular guy in college, whereas people barely looked at her twice. Yet, Rudra had always made her feel special, squashing all her doubts.

'I just wanted to make you feel loved. It was not just to impress you but also to tell you that I have never felt like this before. You know that I have been with a lot of girls, but the effect you have on me is nowhere close to those girls whose beauty is just skin-deep, and they have nothing to contribute to a conversation.'

'How?'

'You are genuinely beautiful and intelligent. You don't fake anything and I love you for that.'

Rudra kissed her hand as he drove to Titos Lane for dinner. The parking lot was just a block away from the restaurant. Rudra got out of the car and went around to open Geet's door and then offered his hand to help her out of the car. He locked the car and they started walking towards Britto's. Geet held his hand and their fingers intertwined. She walked very close to him, hanging on to his hand tightly. Rudra looked down at her and softly touched her lips with his. She kissed him back, eager for more. They entered the restaurant and were warmly greeted by the captain. Their table was ready and they sat down right away. The captain presented him with the wine menu, and Rudra ordered a bottle of white wine without looking.

'Your appetizers would be ready in few minutes, sir. Enjoy the wine while you wait.'

Geet was delighted with Rudra as she enjoyed being courted and treated like a real lady. The captain served fish and prawns for appetizers. Both of them had a good time eating it. Rudra had asked the head steward to pick out the chef's recommended dishes at the time of making the reservation. By doing that, he was assured that he would be treated to a meal that was special and out of the menu. Geet was especially impressed with the way the food was presented. She couldn't stop thanking him for making her dreams a reality. The table was placed on the beach facing the sea with candlelight and was isolated from the others to give them privacy. The soft Goan songs made the ambience very romantic.

Geet extended her hand across the table wanting him to hold it. Rudra reached over and touched her hand gently. She looked down at their hands and then up into his eyes.

'This is the best time I have ever had. I never believed that a guy could treat me so well and bring me to such a wonderful place. I will always remember this as my best date for as long as I live.'

'There are many to follow,' Rudra said, kissing her softly.

'Nevertheless, this will always be the best among them all as it has brought a new light into my life. When we met, I had doubts that you would be everything you portrayed, because I didn't think it was possible to find someone so perfect for me in so many ways. The first day we kissed, I knew this was something special but I did not know I would feel so intensely about you so soon. I love you so much.'

Geet squeezed his hands. She was shedding happy tears. Rudra wanted to catch her tears and preserve them forever. Once they were done with the dinner, they ordered tiramisu for dessert. Rudra signalled to the captain asking for the bill. He smiled and walked away. Geet excused herself and went to the ladies' washroom to freshen up. Rudra got up to speak to the captain.

'The young lady and you look so happy together that the owner and I want this meal to be our gift to you. You have been a good patron to us over the years. It's now time for us to show our gratitude to you.'

All Rudra could say was thanks and shake his hand. Geet was back and he could clearly see the happiness in her eyes and calmness in her soul.

'Should we go for a walk on the beach before I drop you back?' Rudra asked.

'Yes, I will go anywhere you take me,' she said.

She put her hand at the back of his head, pulling him down to her lips, kissing him for a long time. Eventually, they began to walk away. The best feeling in the world is to know that you mean everything to someone.

'Don't go deep inside the water. Stay close to me.' Rudra was worried about Geet as he held on to her arm.

'But I want to.'

'Sssh. Come here.'

Both of them walked a bit and sat down on the sand. Geet was silent for a moment as her heart was pounding hard. She had never been alone on the beach with a guy before. How she wished for time to stop so she could have this happy moment forever.

'When was the first time you felt we could be more than friends?' Geet asked as she played with his jacket.

Rudra responded immediately: 'When you turned back to walk towards your hostel gate after making that remark about my dad. It felt like you knew me somehow and it made me realize how I was running away from myself. Just to prove to myself that love doesn't exist; I played with the feelings of girls by dating them casually. When you pointed out that I was no different from my dad, your depth of understanding and honesty impressed me.'

'So don't you think you should talk to him once? After all, we are sitting here because of him. If you had not told me his story, then I wouldn't have had that insight which triggered the feelings in you.' Geet moved closer to him to convince him to call his dad

'No way. That's bizarre. I have not spoken to him for years.'

'Yet, you said you still love him, right?'

They looked at each other with different thoughts for the next few seconds. Rudra thought about it and asked her if she was really serious about it. Geet pointed to his mobile phone and nodded.

Rudra took the phone from her and dialled his father's number. There was no answer. So Geet suggested that he leave a voice message. Rudra called once again and the phone went to voicemail. His eyes were moist as he waited for the beep.

'Dad,' he began with a heavy voice. 'It's me. Rudra. I am sorry for not talking to you for years, I am sorry for thinking that you are the worst dad, but the truth is I love you and I miss you.' Rudra hung up as he couldn't speak more.

Geet kissed him to calm him down and held on to him for a long time.

Rudra smiled and said, 'You can make me smile so easily. I can't lose you because if I ever did, I would lose my best friend, my soulmate, my smile, my laugh, my everything. You bring out the best in me.'

As they started walking on the beach once again, Geet seemed to be lost in thought. Rudra noticed it and asked her if everything was all right. She nodded and assured him that nothing could be wrong with such a beautiful evening. Rudra did not give up so easily, 'Are you crying?'

'No, why? There is no reason to cry.' Geet tried to avoid answering.

'There is nothing wrong with crying.'

'I know there's nothing wrong with crying but I am okay.'

'Really?' Rudra asked suspiciously.

Geet finally gave in and conveyed her thoughts: 'I am just worried about Tushita. I am so happy right now but her life has suddenly changed for the worse, and it is very difficult to see her in the state she is in. Vivaan is helping and encouraging her a lot but I just hope she gets back to her normal life soon.'

'What have the doctors said? Will she ever be able to walk again?'

'If she doesn't exercise regularly in the first few months, then she will never be able to walk as her muscles will atrophy. I don't know the exact medical terms but that's the gist of it. If in the first few months, she exercises regularly, then after a couple of weeks she may even be able to walk with the help of a stick instead of a wheelchair.'

'Don't worry, she will be fine. She just needs a little motivation and I am sure that you and Shibani will help her,' Rudra comforted her.

'Moreover, Shibani hates Vivaan and so every time he comes, he has to be cautious.'

'Why does she hate Vivaan?' Rudra asked curiously.

'She blames him for the accident. It's a long story. She hates all men.'

'Is that so?'

'Yeah.' Geet laughed.

'Lesbian?'

'Shut up!'

She pinched his face playfully and he laughed. He ruffled her hair affectionately.

'There is something odd about Vivaan. I was observing him that night and it seemed like he was not very happy seeing us together. Some awkwardness was clearly visible. You guys have just been friends right?' Rudra enquired.

'Of course. It has never been more than that. We are just good friends and he is anyway closer to Tushita. He had just kissed me to save me from the embarrassment in college once.'

Rudra was still not convinced. He trusted Geet but he felt uneasy about Vivaan. However, he didn't want to spend his time with Geet worrying about Vivaan or anyone else. They spent some time walking and playing on the beach and finally it was time to leave. As he drove her to her hostel, Geet reached over and took his hand and wrapped both of hers around it holding it to her bosom. She was cherishing it like her favourite toy. When Rudra drove off, she kept thinking of the magical time they had spent together. Within a few minutes of reaching her room, she messaged him:

I promise you this, from this day forth: I will love you forever—don't ever doubt that. I will never want anyone else's touch but yours; you make me feel like I am the only woman in the world. You are the only man in this world as far as I am concerned. You are my heart and my soul. I feel as though we were always meant to be together. I have always believed that I had a soulmate out there and now I am sure that is you. I see it every time I look into your eyes and I feel it when you hold me in your arms. I love you so much. These five words have more meaning than the meanings of all the words in the world. I love you with all that I am. I love you for all that you are.

Indeed, true love is not coming together of two souls, but it is one incomplete soul finding its other half to live a complete life.

Karmasutra: When Life F**ks You

Next morning, when Geet told Tushita about her relationship she was delighted for her. Tushita had always wanted Geet to find happiness in love. She knew the agony Geet had gone through in her life and thus her happiness had no bounds when she heard about Geet and Rudra. However, her new relationship status didn't go down well with Shibani. Her reaction was unenthusiastic. No doubt, she was concerned for her. Tushita was suffering because of one wrong decision and she didn't want Geet to repeat the mistake. Geet knew that, in time, Shibani would come around to seeing Rudra as the lovely person she knew he was. Until then, she decided to live in the moment, laugh off their concerns and love her friends knowing that everything happened for a reason.

It had almost been a week and now none of the girls in the popular gang tried to pull Geet's leg. On the other hand, Shibani became more and more concerned for Geet. She was not happy with the closeness Geet shared with Rudra and was worried for her. In the past week, she had seen Vivaan taking care of Tushita and inspiring her to live once again. This softened her attitude towards Vivaan. Tushita felt lucky to have Vivaan in her life but she had been careful to express her love for Vivaan only on the pages of her diary, because she had sensed that Vivaan considered her a friend and nothing more.

Vivaan too was not happy with Geet's decision to be with Rudra since he felt left out. However, deep down, they all knew that their friendship was strong and they would always be there for each other.

Geet was just chatting with Tushita while Shibani was completely engrossed with work on her laptop.

'Hey, did you give Tushita the medicines?' Geet asked Shibani.

'No. Can you please do it? I am stuck with work,' Shibani requested.

Geet got the medicines from the drawer and gave it to Tushita along with a glass of water. Tushita was asking

Geet about Rudra and her first kiss but Geet was trying to change the topic.

'Did you guys even make out? How was it, who took charge?' Tushita continued with the trail of questions.

'Shut up!'

Geet kept fobbing Tushita's questions as she blushed at the memory of her intimate moments with Rudra. Her phone beeped:

> Rudra: *Did you submit the project report to that idiotic bald man?*
> Geet: *It was kind of lame but I got laid for it.*
> Rudra: *Laid? WTF.*
> Geet: *OMG. HA HA HA. I mean paid. Autocorrect sucks.*
> Rudra: *Ha ha. I don't understand how autocorrect comes up with so many inappropriate penises.*
> Rudra: **Phrases. ROFL. I am turning this thing off right away.*

Geet couldn't control her laughter any more and showed the chat to Tushita who also began laughing hysterically. Shibani was still engrossed in her work.

Later, when Geet was about to go to bed, she received an email notification of an e-card. She was surprised and secretly pleased. She guessed that Rudra might have sent it.

She tried calling him a couple of times but he didn't pick up. He wasn't online on chat either. She tried to click on the link:

'An e-card full of love is waiting for you.'

She couldn't see the sender's name. It wasn't visible and instead of the e-card opening, she got the message: *No result found*.

Irritated with the process of opening the letter, she texted Rudra and told him that she was not able to open it. When no reply came even after half an hour, Geet retired for the night after putting her phone on silent and on charge.

'Geet . . . wake up . . . Geet!' Tushita was screaming.

Geet woke up with a start.

'What the hell is wrong with you? It's just 7 a.m.,' Geet said, rubbing her eyes as she lay on her bed still half asleep.

'Get up and check your Facebook account!' Tushita continued to scream at the top of her voice.

Shibani was still asleep. After finishing her work, she had slept late. Geet grabbed her mobile, and her heart was in her mouth when she saw there were seventy-five missed calls on it. *Oh my god! Was Rudra all right? Did he have a car accident last night? Was something wrong in the family? Mom, Dad, or someone else? No, that's not possible. Rudra . . . Rudra . . . shit! It has to be something related to him.*

She saw hundreds of Facebook notifications. What she saw gave her the shock of her life. They were nasty messages about her character. She froze when she saw what was posted on her timeline.

Shibani woke up with the noise Tushita and Geet were making. Shibani shook Geet out of her state of shock. There was a post with candid photographs of her and Rudra in intimate positions. These photographs were only meant for their personal use. Geet clearly remembered she had not accessed Facebook the previous night. Her laptop was at the service centre and the network on her phone had not been great, so she hadn't bothered with Facebook at all the previous night. She slowly read the caption of the photographs: *Tips to become popular in college within a few days. Hook up with a popular guy. Be in an open relationship and stay free to hook up with more. I can please anyone in ways you cannot imagine. Message me on . . .*

Her mobile number was clearly uploaded and the post had been shared by many on their own timelines. That explained the sea of notifications. She took a screenshot of the post and deleted the post immediately but the damage had been done. She sat down in one corner of the room, staring blankly at a wall while Shibani and Tushita tried to speak to her. She was shedding tears of sadness. Then she began screaming her lungs out in anger and shame. She was confused about what exactly had happened and who could have done something like this. Who was the one who had crushed her heart and left her to bleed alone?

She called Rudra with tears in her eyes but he didn't pick up the call even after continuous attempts. Shibani and Tushita both started blaming Rudra for the entire act as he was the only one who had been in possession of the photographs and Geet's Facebook password.

'Remember, I had told you to be careful? All men are bloody cheap and I told you to stay away from dickheads.' Shibani expressed her anger.

'He loved you right? Do you think this is a prank?' Tushita asked in a soft tone.

Geet glanced at both of them and called Rudra once again but there was no answer. Her heart didn't believe that Rudra could do something so horrible but after listening to Shibani and Tushita, her mind began considering the possibility. The demons of darkness had driven her to the bridge of fear making her feel ugly. She wanted to run away but to find out the truth, she decided to go to college and face the storm. She wanted to know why Rudra had played with her feelings and thrown her like garbage on the road, alone and wounded.

Tushita asked Shibani to accompany Geet to the college so that she wouldn't have to face the gossipmongers alone.

'Please don't worry. Everything will be fine and keep messaging me,' Tushita said in concern.

The only thing that hurts worse than your own pain is seeing the one you love in pain, knowing that you can't do anything to help them. Tushita wanted to go along with her but her physical state didn't permit her to do so. As they reached the college gate, Geet slowed down her pace taking small steps in apprehension of what lay ahead. As expected, the popular girls' group was waiting to ridicule her. Shibani held her hand firmly and walked through the entrance. Geet couldn't gather enough courage to even look up. Shibani was trying her best to make sure that no one pointed fingers at her friend but it was becoming impossible to protect her against the sheer number of detractors.

'The queen, THE POPULAR GIRL of the college, is here. Welcome her, friends.'

'Her mind acts like Google but her multitalented lusty self wants guys to ogle.'

The remarks continued until Shibani threatened them. 'You haven't forgotten the slap, have you?' she yelled.

Geet felt depressed even though none of this was her fault. Her only fault was that she had trusted someone blindly.

As they reached the inner campus, Vivaan came running towards Geet complaining that he had been trying her mobile phone since morning. He had also tried contacting Shibani and Tushita but had got no response.

'Everyone is disturbed, let's not get hung up on little things,' Shibani said, trying to avoid him.

'Who's done this? I am sure Geet hasn't posted it. I wonder if it is the girls from the popular gang—' Vivaan was speculating when Shibani interrupted him rudely, 'How can you be so sure? Maybe 'you know who' is behind this,' Shibani added angrily.

Vivaan didn't react to Shibani's statement but looked worried for Geet. He knew the popular girls were jealous of Geet since she had started dating Rudra, and suspected that they might have been behind it. Vivaan could see that Geet had become really quiet and her eyes were seeking Rudra in the crowd. She could not believe Rudra could be the mastermind behind it. She knew their love was real when she had looked into his eyes and had been enveloped in his arms. She believed that the moment he spotted her, he would come running and hug her.

Then she saw him. He was standing right there, surrounded by his classmates. As soon as Geet saw him, she rushed towards him, but when he saw her, he turned and started walking the other way. Geet was shocked! She had expected him to be with her and support her in such a situation. All of a sudden, her faith in him shrank and disbelief took over her mind. She caught up with him and stopped him with her arm and broke her long silence. 'What was my fault? Was it that I loved you and had blind faith in you? What was it? It's so easy for you to walk away when you know the situation. I have been trying your to reach your phone since morning but you seem to be too busy to care. I loved you, I had dreamt of living my life with you. Then why? Isn't it your responsibility to be with me when I need someone to support me emotionally? A relationship is all about being happy together and about fighting the difficulties together, not about being in bed together. Where do you turn when the person you need the most doesn't care enough to hold you when you are in pain?'

Rudra didn't utter a word and just kept gazing at her.

'Speak up!' Shibani screamed at him as she stood beside Geet.

Vivaan stood there holding Geet to comfort her.

Rudra snatched Geet's hand that Vivaan was holding and took her to a corner of the campus that was a bit more secluded. Vivaan didn't like the way he dominated Geet and nor did Shibani. He also instructed both Vivaan and Shibani to stay away for some time. They agreed only when Geet told them that she would be back. Rudra took her to the other corner, tugging painfully at her arm.

'Have you lost it? First, you upload the photos from your own profile tagging me in them and then you blame me for uploading them? Hats off to your tricks! You wanted a deal so that you could become popular, and like a fool I thought you loved me too. I was completely wrong.'

'You didn't . . . ?'

'Why should I? If you have forgotten, then let me remind you that I had deleted those pictures in front of you the last time we met. From where am I supposed to upload them? Who do you think you are? Without even thinking once, you blame me in front of everyone pretending to be innocent. Didn't you feel ashamed of yourself when you uploaded your number or were you so drowned in your ego completely to care? How badly did you want to prove to those girls that you are a player? Just fuck off from here. I don't want to see your face. The way you deleted the photos from Facebook, delete me from your life too. It's over and I am very clear about it. Don't try to drag me into your life any more.' Rudra left after saying what he wanted to.

'Rudra!' Geet tried to stop him but couldn't. She realized what a blunder she had made by putting the blame on him. She recollected that he had deleted the photos from his mobile and had asked her to delete it too, but she had been lazy about it.

Rudra must have been taken aback when he saw the post in the morning, and in his rage, he must have decided to stay away from Geet after misinterpreting her intentions. That is why when he had seen Geet coming towards him, he had started walking away to avoid talking in front of everyone else. Relationships require simple things—honesty, communication, loyalty, trust and love. If you lack any of these, you are left with nothing. When Geet showed distrust, he immediately decided never to bother with Geet again. Breaking up is never easy. To cleanse all the emotions that were injected in your body through the syringe of love is more difficult than clearing up blood affected by drugs. Rudra blocked her on every social media forums. They could have tried to make it work but he decided to maintain a distance to avoid complications. Sometimes what holds you together and what tears you apart are the same things.

Geet did not even get a chance to explain. One impulsive decision of hers had led to the end of a budding relationship that could have flowered beautifully. Geet was lost in tears as she realized that she had done the best she could have, but it had still not been enough. She remembered how they had started talking; she had trusted him with the things that she had trusted anyone else with, and now he was gone. You can never control your feelings, but feelings can control you and keep you caged. The worst feeling is feeling unwanted by the person you want the most. She kept trying to understand how someone could access her profile so easily when no one had the password other than Rudra, but she remained completely clueless.

Rudra was not involved in it; of this, she was quite sure. Yet, the question remained unanswered and the mystery unsolved. Who would do this, and why? Love and life are like one big jigsaw puzzle; on some days the pieces go together perfectly while on other days they just don't seem to fit at all.

She Can't Even Think Straight

How could you think that I would cause any harm to your character? I can still remember your face when you had so confidently said that we would stay together forever. Are 'forever' and 'ever' just words? You made me feel complete and showed me how to love unconditionally, and I know that no one can now make me feel this way. I thought I had finally found someone true but I was wrong. My love for you won't die easily. I wish you would open your eyes and look at me and hear, 'I love you and I don't want to let you go.

Rudra was sitting alone in his apartment, thinking of Geet and remembering the memories he had shared with Geet in the same room. He kept pondering over the incident that had taken place. Once again, he checked the screenshot he had taken. When he observed carefully, he realized that there was no mention on the post that the photos had been uploaded from a mobile phone. This meant that they had been uploaded from either a desktop or a laptop. It was also clear to him that Geet had neither of them last night. Damn. Had he jumped to a conclusion too quickly? He now understood why she was blaming him the way she had. The more he thought about who could be the culprit, the clearer his doubts became. He remembered how Vivaan looked heartbroken when they were together at the club and during the following days. He concluded that Vivaan had feelings for Geet and thus had systematically planned a trap so that Geet and Rudra would drift apart. With every thought, his doubt about Vivaan became stronger and he rushed to meet him in college, burning with anger.

'Vivaan!' Rudra shouted as he saw Vivaan outside the college campus.

Vivaan looked around but couldn't spot the source of the sound. 'Turn back. I am here,' Rudra ordered.

Vivaan turned and saw Rudra standing there, livid with anger. Clueless about what was coming his way, he greeted Rudra as he approached him. As they stood face-to-face, both stared at each other without blinking. Before any of them could utter a word, Rudra punched him with full force. Vivaan lost his balance and took a step back to regain his composure. He was staring at Rudra in disbelief. 'What the fuck, you . . .' Vivaan muttered

From the corner of his eye, he saw Rudra's other arm approach him in an upward trajectory. He ducked this time. The blow was meant for his jaw, but since he was trying to duck, it caught his nose and Vivaan's nose broke in the impact. Rudra was shouting, 'Why did you upload Geet's photos? If you had a problem with me, you should have dealt with me,' Rudra shouted, holding Vivaan's hair in one hand.

'What is wrong with you?' Vivaan said.

Rudra was about to hit him again but this time Vivaan threw his forearms in defence and pushed Rudra's elbow down and away. He caught hold of his head and pushed him on to the floor. It continued for the next few minutes in the middle of the road and Vivaan punched him constantly in self-defence. 'Rudra . . . we can talk. I haven't done anything,' Vivaan said, trying to breathe as he was badly bruised and his tooth was also knocked out.

Rudra's hands too were sore and he took a deep breath. He had hurt his ribcage. He inhaled and exhaled again, struggled to put his arms under him and pushed himself up on his hands and knees. As he got up, it hurt his ribs some more, and so he stayed that way for a bit, on his hands and knees with his head hanging like a horse. He crawled over and got hold of the bench beside him and slowly managed to sit upright. Vivaan came and sat beside him and gave him a bottle of water. Rudra took a sip and started to feel better.

'It's not me. She is a good friend. I know what you must be thinking but I just get really worried about her as Tushita is already suffering. My worries were not without reason. Look at what has happened now,' Vivaan said, regaining his breath.

Vivaan explained everything about their relationship and how it was nothing more than pure friendship. Rudra, who was sure that Vivaan had been behind all this, was now absolutely confused. He couldn't decide if Vivaan was actually expressing himself or trying to distract him from the truth. He decided to find out for himself, without telling Geet. Though he wasn't very convinced, he decided to go with Vivaan's story for the time being before he could find out the truth behind this cruel act.

If you have true feelings for someone, those feelings never really go away, no matter what the provocation. Geet loved Rudra and had not gotten over her feelings for him, but the way their relationship had ended, she was shattered from within. She had expected Rudra to understand her and feel her agony, but he hadn't even bothered to hear her out. He had neither messaged nor called. Every time her phone vibrated, she thought it was him but she was always disappointed. Rudra had blocked her completely from his life. Even after she had changed her phone number, she had tried reaching him but had not been able to. In this tough time, Tushita and Shibani stood firmly by her and tried to help her get over him. It wasn't easy. She had surrendered her life to him and had never imagined a moment without him.

Geet couldn't stop herself and tried to contact him one more time. She messaged:

I wish I could just learn to forget your smile and the moments we shared. You taught me how to handle myself when everything gets tough, but you forgot to teach me how to stand on my own without you. It seems like you are content without me. How could you doubt my words when I said I loved you? I'm sensitive, I overthink every little thing and I care way too much. I love you more than you'll ever know. Now you have simply changed and that breaks my heart into pieces. Yet, despite all we've been through, I can't learn to hate and forget you. My feelings for you were true and will always remain the same. I am really sorry if I have hurt you.

The message was delivered successfully as he didn't have her new number, so he couldn't have blocked the number. Geet stared at the screen and her heart skipped a beat when she saw Rudra online. He remained online. Her hopes were shattered once again when he decided not to reply. Instead, he blocked her new number too.

The hardest thing is to go on with your life without the one person whom you thought would be constant throughout your life. Geet had no choice. Everything she did reminded her of Rudra. Vivaan had told her about his attack, but her love for him was unshakeable. Vivaan tried talking to her when he had come to the hostel to meet Tushita but Geet was lost in her own world of pain. Hence, in order to not upset her further, he left with Tushita to go around the hostel grounds like he always did. Before closing the door, Tushita glanced at Geet, expecting her to say something but she didn't. Despite Shibani and Tushita trying their best to cheer her up, there was something missing. Anyone can make you smile but only a few can make you happy, and Geet's happiness was gone along with Rudra.

> *Why has everything gone so wrong? Have I messed up? I am losing everyone I love. I am losing myself. I feel like I am fragmenting, dissolving into something unknown. Words can make or break a person's spirit. I wonder how much more of this pain I can take.*

Geet was staring constantly at the bottle of vodka that she had been drinking for quite some time. It was midafternoon and Shibani finally broke her trance when she shook her by the shoulders. 'Are you okay? Should I get you something?' Shibani asked, sitting beside Geet and pouring a drink for herself too.

Geet just nodded; she was quite drunk by then. She had never imagined that her life would take such a turn but no one really has control over fate.

'Make me one more drink, neat,' Geet managed to say, pointing at the bottle.

It was not the first time she was drinking but she had never gotten so drunk before. She had the drink in one go and winced as it burnt her throat. They both continued to drink in companionable silence until they had finished the entire bottle. Vivaan and Tushita were still not back in the room. Shibani could see that Geet was completely drunk as she had started slurring, and at one point she also made some random remarks about Rudra. Shibani was high too but not as drunk as Geet. Geet tried to move but could only manage to roll over the bed with Shibani's help.

She asked Shibani in her slurred voice to put lotion near her thighs which had been hurting her for quite some time. Shibani began to rub the ointment on the pink and tender skin of her thighs. She kept massaging it while Geet thanked her, her face buried in her pillow. She slowly reached up and asked her if she could massage a little higher.

'Yeah . . . there . . . that's where it hurts . . . I think,' Geet remarked in her drunken stupor.

Shibani felt an emotion she had never felt for Geet before. She had felt like this once but today it felt more intense. She found herself staring at the lower half of Geet's naked rear. Her hands were only inches away from Geet's vagina. Alcohol acted like a catalyst for her abandonment. She took a moment to admire her lovely skin and the dark curves of her genital crack imagining what lay between.

Slowly she began massaging Geet, rubbing the uppermost part of her thigh, just below the left cheek of her bottom. Despite the liquor, Shibani could feel her pulse race because of the new experience. It didn't take her long to realize that Geet was also unaware of just who was touching her because of the alcohol. Her occasional murmurs turned into soft moans of satisfaction. Instinctively, Geet parted her legs a bit more and pressed her warm vulva against Shibani's hand.

Shibani could feel her wetness and knew immediately that she was aroused. Much to her surprise, so was Shibani. For a brief moment there was absolute silence in the room. The only sound that could be heard was that of the ticking clock. Shibani ran her fingers up and down the lips and felt her wetness. She touched it gently. Geet began to thrust her hips, arching her back for more contact. Shibani responded by inserting her finger into her wet loveliness.

'Ohhhh . . . it feels amazing . . . ohhh,' Geet moaned, she had lost herself to the sensation.

Shibani couldn't believe how turned on she was by feeling another girl so intimately and seeing her respond with such obvious sexual excitement. It was unreal. Her head was spinning. She moved her fingers in and out rhythmically until Geet grew wetter and moaned even louder with her face buried in the pillow. Despite her own increasing excitement, Shibani concentrated on pleasing Geet and began thrusting in and out rapidly, replicating the rhythm of a man. She removed the pillow. Geet's eyes were still closed. There was an awkward silence between them as Shibani moved closer to her.

'Your legs are way too sexy,' Shibani whispered, stroking her arm with one hand.

'Your . . . everything about you is sexy,' Geet mumbled.

'I find you so interesting. It's your lips. They got me. I just want to pin you down and kiss them. I don't even want you to kiss me back; I just want to suck them.'

Holy fucking shit, Shibani thought as she lost control over her words.

Their lips connected eagerly but Geet was responding as if on autopilot mode. After a while, she too started to tongue-wrestle, fighting for dominance. Shibani sucked her bottom lip while running her hands all over her body.

'You look so good in my arms,' Shibani muttered again.

'Mmmm . . . we should stop,' Geet managed to say.

Shibani continued her assault on her lips as Geet moaned softly. Soon Shibani began to feel Geet losing control as she felt her hips shudder yet again. Between the alcohol and her beating heart, Shibani felt incredibly dizzy from what had just happened. Somewhat embarrassed, she mumbled that she had to go to bed. Geet muttered something indistinctly. Shibani just hoped that everything would be forgotten when she woke up. She slept on the bed beside her and lowered her shorts and panties under the blanket. She held the fingers that had just been soaked in Geet's wetness under her nose, breathing in the sexual musk as she relieved herself for the first time. A thundering orgasm followed but even before the waves of desire had fully subsided, she fell into a deep, satisfied sleep.

An hour later, Shibani suddenly woke up. She had no idea what time it was and was a bit shocked to find herself lying half-naked on the bed, until she remembered what had happened before she had fallen asleep. She glanced around to see if Vivaan and Tushita were back but to her relief, they were not around. Pulling up her panties and shorts under the blanket, she looked at Geet who was not in her bed. Shibani could hear her throwing up in the washroom. Shibani went in and kneeled down and wiped Geet's face. Geet looked at her and asked in a husky voice if she could help her to the bed. Geet didn't even talk about what had happened before she had fallen asleep. She didn't remember anything. Shibani felt a great sense of relief. While Geet was settling down, Shibani called Tushita to enquire about her whereabouts. Tushita was just outside the hostel, sitting and talking. Shibani checked the time and realized that it was not even late evening yet. Once Geet managed to sit properly, Shibani helped her lift her spoiled gown to change as some vomit had stained her gown. She found herself looking at the rest of her body. In that soft light, Shibani thought she looked incredibly attractive.

Shibani had never had such strong feelings for anyone, and today when she had felt them, they had been for a girl. Of all the people she could feel attracted to, it was her best friend Geet she had feelings for. It felt real. It was not just physical for her any more. All she could think of was Geet. She was surprised that she had not come to terms with her sexual orientation before today. Sometimes all you need is that one person who shows you that it's okay to let your guard down, be yourself and love with no regrets. As she lay beside Geet, a volcano of thoughts and desires flooded her mind.

Forgive my fingers for when they find your body, when they lose themselves. Do you realize what you do to me? Why can you not understand me? I listen to my heart but it does not know what to do. I listen to my head, but my mind is so confused. I like you. I need you. I want you. How long will this last? Will we remain friends when it is all over? When it is over, will we still have forever?

Don't Hate Me for Who I Am

A loving boyfriend would never give up on his girlfriend despite any differences that may have cropped up between them. Rudra had no intention of giving up on Geet, especially after knowing that she was innocent. Though he had ignored Geet for the last few days, with each passing day he was getting more desperate to get her back. Yet, he knew he had to focus completely on sorting out something else first. With the help of some friends who were good with computers, he was trying to trace the person who had hacked into Geet's accounts. He had provided the details of Geet's accounts on both Facebook and Gmail. He had a niggling doubt that Vivaan was somehow involved and wanted the truth to be out as soon as possible, at any cost. The tech-savvy friends were on the trail, and discovered that a night before, a greeting card had been sent to Geet's email. When she clicked on it, it activated an identity-theft virus. It provided remote access to the user and all the security details from the phone through which she accessed it. His friends also revealed that the IP address did not match the hostel's, and suspected that someone from outside had done it. It was very evident by then that the same person who had sent the email had uploaded the photographs. However, as the mail was spam, it did not have a valid user email address.

Every computer has an internet protocol address through which he or she can be traced easily by professionals. All that was needed was a little more time to crack this mystery.

Rudra waited patiently for the details thinking about Geet and the moments they had spent together. She had touched his heart in the most amazing ways. He missed her sincerity and vibrancy. He missed their night-long talks on nothing specific, their personal conversations and their silly little fights. You never really forget the ones who truly touched your heart; whether they're the ones who broke it or the ones who healed it.

Walking alone is not painful but when we have walked a mile with someone, walking alone can become unbearable.

Nothing seemed to make Geet feel better and she made drinking in the afternoon a habit. She constantly missed college. She didn't have the heart to face anyone and avoided attending lectures and workshops. Shibani used to come early to give Geet company when she was alone in the room. As usual, Tushita used to go out with Vivaan. Even in isolation, Shibani used to go through a range of emotions while trying to hide her feelings from Geet.

Geet was drunk. Not as much as the other day but certainly tipsy. As they sat beside each other, their shoulders touched. Shibani could feel the warmth of her body and could also feel her breath. She started rubbing Geet's bare thighs below her skirt. Geet had no clue about Shibani's intentions so she didn't say anything in the beginning but when it continued, she asked, 'What are you doing?'

'Do you like it?' Shibani leaned closer to her face as she kept rolling her fingers on her thighs moving slightly upwards.

Geet didn't respond this time and Shibani kept advancing. Shibani was not as drunk as the other day but her feelings were as intense as they had been on the day she had discovered the truth about her sexuality. She was very attracted to Geet and it was getting difficult to control her emotions around her. She even considered telling Geet about the other day but there was a part of her that just couldn't take that chance. Shibani was Geet's secret admirer. It was the most appropriate term she could think of. Geet was on her mind all the time. Maybe it was the way she looked after her transformation. Maybe it was Geet's incredible brain. Shibani could not put her finger on what she liked the most about Geet but she certainly could not deny the sexual attraction she felt for her.

'I am so glad that you are exercising,' Vivaan commented as he sat along with Tushita outside the hostel gate.

'I don't know if I can recover completely but I am grateful to god for bringing you into my life,' Tushita remarked.

'I am sure you will recover soon.'

'Thanks. These days I am worried about Geet. I just don't know how to help her,' Tushita said, biting her nails.

'Give her some time. Things will get better.'

'I can't believe someone would actually want her life to become a living hell,' Tushita looked at Vivaan.

Vivaan didn't react. After a brief silence, he stood up to take Tushita back to the hostel. That's when they noticed Rudra speeding towards them in his car. He parked the car in a rush and with a bitter look in his eyes walked towards them.

'I need to meet Geet right now.'

Vivaan replied in a disinterested tone, 'I will inform her that you are here. She is in the room with Shibani.'

They both started walking towards the gate when Rudra grabbed Vivaan's shoulder and ordered him to take him inside along with him. Vivaan, however, was worried that the warden would object. Rudra was adamant. The warden allowed Vivaan to come and go because she knew Vivaan was Tushita's close friend and was helping her recover. Vivaan finally decided to take the risk. However, they got lucky because the warden was not around and the security person didn't question them because Vivaan was a regular guest. Rudra had found out about the person who had uploaded the photos and had tried to create a drift between them but he wanted to talk to Geet first to avoid further complications. Fear engulfed Vivaan when he saw Rudra's dark expression and with each step he took towards the room, he became more anxious. Tushita, too, was taken aback and sensed trouble. Rudra's eyes expressed many things at that moment. 'Do you have the keys? Geet might be sleeping,' Vivaan questioned Tushita as they stood in front of the door.

'Yes,' Tushita took it out and handed it to Vivaan.

As Vivaan opened the door, they all almost screamed in shock. Geet and Shibani were in each other's arms and were smooching. Shibani was leaning forward with her hands around Geet's neck lost in bliss as they sat in front of each other on the floor. Geet, on the other hand, had rested her hands on Shibani's thighs, responding to the kiss with her eyes closed.

'Di! What the hell are you doing? Are you fucking insane?' Tushita screamed, turning her face away.

Both Shibani and Geet came back to their senses and were horrified to see everyone. Shibani looked down in guilt and Geet looked shocked by her own behaviour. In her intoxicated state, she had encouraged Shibani to proceed unknowingly. On seeing Rudra, she seemed to have been jolted into sobriety and was filled with regret. She stood numb. Vivaan closed the door and stood next to Rudra, unsettled by what he had just witnessed. Tushita was still shocked.

'I . . . I don't know what happened . . . I was not even aware of what I was . . . shit . . . what the hell was I doing? I am hammered . . . I was lost in the flow . . . I thought Rudra was kissing me,' Geet tried to explain.

'I don't want to hear anything. You both were actually . . . I don't even feel like saying what you were doing. When did this happen? Despo . . . Di . . . you too, what made you? Just because you hate men doesn't mean you would behave like this.' Tushita could barely articulate her thoughts, she was so shocked.

Vivaan had sat down on the bed. 'Geet . . . what is happening? Is this a phase or are you lost? Whatever it is, you just need to figure it out. In the last few days, you have gone completely haywire. Your focus only used to be studies but in the last few months you have faked a boyfriend, then changed your avatar, uploaded your own photographs on Facebook and are now kissing Shibani.'

Shibani sat there with her head hung in shame. Geet was sobbing, but Rudra was the one who broke the silence, 'Geet did not upload the photos.' He said.

Geet immediately looked up at Rudra with relief in her eyes.

'What?' Tushita was shocked.

'Then who did it?' Vivaan asked.

Rudra looked at Vivaan and reluctantly apologized for getting into a fight with him. Geet wiped away her tears and Rudra stepped towards her with an apologetic look.

'Who did it and why?' Geet asked as Rudra leaned over and gave her his hands to hold and lifted her up slowly.

'I now understand why it was done,' Rudra stated, and then, yelling at the top of his voice, he added, 'You should probably ask this bitch, Shibani.'

'Have you gone nuts, Rudra? Are you blaming my sister?' Tushita reacted instinctively protective of her sibling.

'What the fuck?' Vivaan exclaimed.

Geet froze when she heard this.

'Yes, Shibani.'

Shibani looked up towards Geet who was so drunk that Rudra had to support her to stay upright. Geet felt as if her world was falling apart. Shibani had been her best friend. In fact, she had been more than a friend; she had been like her sister. She could not believe the enormity of what Shibani had done. Tushita and Vivaan were dumbstruck. No one wanted to believe it and every heart was broken.

Rudra yelled at Shibani, asking her to speak up, but she just stared at everyone without saying a word. The expressions on everyone's faces consumed her from within. She thought explaining would be pointless because no one would understand Shibani. She was like a puzzle going through a storm and she needed someone to tell her that she was not alone in this. Yet, she was. When everyone demanded an answer from her, she finally spoke.

'What should a person do when it feels like there is no one to understand her agony? How do you face the confusion and the fear of dejection? Will you hate me if I come out of the closet? Yes, I uploaded the photos on Facebook through Geet's profile. It was not for revenge. I was possessed and not thinking straight. I am still trying to figure out my reason behind it. Was it insecurity or pure jealously? I do not know. Will we remain friends once you hear my confession? I doubt it. The truth is that I am still trying to figure out who I am.

'When I saw you closely after your makeover, there was an instant attraction, a sensation that had never hit me before. I just glanced at your reflection in the mirror of my bike and that was a terrible mistake because I got lost. When you told me about your relationship, I felt possessive, but will you throw me out of your life for that? What was I supposed to do to control my true feelings? No, I didn't expect you to feel anything other than friendship or sisterly love for me, but on the other hand, I was scared of losing a friend like you.

'We always talked about Rudra and that made me very unhappy. I have always hated men but no one has ever asked me the reason behind it. With our every action, there is a reason behind them. My reason was Tushita's ex-boyfriend. I have seen him hurt her badly, both physically and emotionally. Before this, I had seen my dad hit my mom brutally and I had heard her cry herself to sleep every night. I had felt her pain. It strengthened my belief that all men were the same.

'They treat us like slaves and playthings. They think they can show dominance because they are men. I never stopped anyone from talking to guys but I preferred to stay away from them personally. How could I have loved them? Just give me one reason, will you? Men have given nothing but pain to my mum and my sister. I realized how cruel men are. It didn't end there. Despite warning Tushita, she fell in love with Andy. One day he slapped her, the other day he punched her, then he flung her down. Why? Just because of his ego? What was my sister's fault? He became more and more violent and that triggered my senses. I hate men and I have no shame in saying it.

'But I never realized that this outrage for them would grow so intense that I would start feeling things for Geet. I started liking her but as soon as I did, she revealed to me that she was in a relationship. I felt shattered, scared and insecure all over again. Not just because I liked her and had developed feelings for her but also because I didn't want Tushita's story to repeat itself. Even your most casual conflict felt like mountains to me because they reminded me of the path my sister had chosen to take. I wanted to separate you both.

'That night when I was working on my laptop, I was actually chatting with a friend who is a hacker. She helped me create an identity-theft virus that I mailed to Geet. I got access and all security logins through cookies once she clicked on the greeting card link. I didn't use hostel Wi-Fi to avoid getting into trouble and instead used my mobile hotspot. I had already copied the photos from your laptop some days ago. I didn't want to lose you. When I look at Tushita on this wheelchair, I am overwhelmed with sadness and pain. She is my life and her pain paralyses my heart. I never knew what I did would affect you and your relationship in such a drastic manner. I feel guilty, but if this would not have happened, then I would have never realized and accepted who I am. Yes, I am a lesbian.

'I realized it the afternoon when you and I were completely drunk. That evening when you had asked me if something had happened before you went off to sleep, I had lied. We had come very close. Our closeness had crossed all limits that day. Since that day, I have been thinking about who I am. I have always felt more inclined towards girls and when I searched online, I discovered that there are many like me out there. It seems strange but it is extremely normal. There are teachers, doctors, celebrities—there are people who are single, people who are married, people who are mothers and daughters, and they all feel it. I then realized that there is nothing wrong with it. It was my choice to either pretend to live my life as a lie or accept my true feelings.

'I never openly spoke to anybody about my feelings. I never had a girlfriend but there is no way I can deny these feelings that I seem to be having. I am a lesbian, not a vampire. I won't harm anyone. I am not a contagious disease. I am human and I apologize for what I did. They were a result of my own insecurities. Geet, will you still be my friend and accept me? Tushita, would you forgive your sister?'

Love Doesn't Have an Expiry Date

Life is very unpredictable, blessed one moment and crushed in the next. Shibani felt like she had been robbed but wasn't sure what it was that she had been robbed of. Her strength, her belief or her identity? She had stopped running away from her feelings and had accepted them despite knowing that it wasn't going to be easy for her. Yet, what she had not anticipated was that she would now have to walk alone without even the support of her closed ones. She missed her mom. At this confusing time, her unconditional love was all she would have needed to make sense of the world again. With every passing minute, she was consumed with guilt. She wanted to scratch her skin to get rid of the feeling of being seen as dirty. Geet wasn't willing to utter a word to her and slept at a considerable distance from her. There had been times when Shibani had stood up for Geet but when she needed her friend, Geet was nowhere near her. Rudra had exposed the truth and ignored her in college. Vivaan was the only one who didn't show any objection but it didn't really matter as Shibani was not very fond of him. Shibani had stayed with Tushita in the hardest of times but even Tushita had left her alone after coming to know that her sister was a lesbian.

Sitting alone she pondered:

How do I explain to these people that I have not changed? I am still the same human being who loves them, cares for them and would support them no matter what. I agree that I made a mistake but I was fighting my own emotions, struggling between reality and belief. My one confession has made me taboo. This is not right. What can I do if I can't even think straight? A straight man feels attracted towards a woman and that's perfectly normal. Similarly, I feel attracted towards girls—how is that my fault? How do I explain to them that I still love them?

We have a tendency to looking at things within our limited boundaries. Anything that is not set within those fixed boundaries is signed off as a disease. Sometimes, such limitations create a dispute in the society and take you away from your loved ones. Shibani was facing something similar.

She felt like her world was crashing down around her. Her heart ached but she didn't give up on her soul. It had not been her choice but that was the way she was. All she wanted was someone to hold her, someone to comfort her, someone to love her for what she was. Was that too much to ask?

'Is everything sorted between Rudra and you?' Tushita asked as they both ate.

'Not really. There is still some distance. We are not together like before,' Geet said, munching her salad.

'I think you should apologize for the distrust you showed.'

'He could have done that too,' Geet said, looking up at her.

'He didn't leave you alone, Geet. He fought to prove your innocence. He was the one who had made you believe in yourself. Don't let ego come in between you both when there is space for love,' Tushita advised.

Tushita was not wrong and Geet knew that. They had not met after Shibani's confession and a couple of days had passed since that incident. They had exchanged smiles but that was all. Geet agreed to take the first step because she did not want to let go of the person who despite knowing all her flaws had loved her unconditionally. She messaged him:

I wonder why you chose me and why you are with me. I know we've gone through a lot. We have had hard times, but we have also had good times. We don't always share the same things but there is an understanding between us. A look into your eyes is enough to tell me much you love me and how much you care about me. It took me a few days away from you to realize it but now I understand. When you asked me if I trusted you, I looked for reasons not to and I found none. I know we have both been hurt and have lost trust in each other but I ask you to give me a chance, the same way I am willing to give you one. I don't ask for much, only for you to love me as I am. I only wish to be by your side and with no one else. I am sorry but I can't stop loving you. Will you please love me like you did before?

The moment Geet sent him a message, he replied:

Let's meet. I am in college. I can give you as many chances as you want because you give me a reason to live. I love you. Come soon.

Geet blushed in excitement and rushed to college. Love is a simple four-letter word. Yet, it's not so simple. It can confuse feelings, ruin friendships or start new ones. For

Geet, love was what made everything appear positive and bright. The moment she reached college and saw Rudra, she hugged him. 'I have missed you. I have missed you so much. Nobody can imagine how much I have missed you.'

'I am sorry,' Rudra said, kissing her forehead.

Geet had tears in her eyes as she said, 'I know I don't tell you often that I love you, but as the days go by, my love for you grows, and each day I thank god that I have you in my life. I know I get mad and upset. It is because my love for you is so strong that it scares me.'

'I am not going anywhere. I purposely didn't try to get in touch as I wanted to find out the truth first. I knew you were innocent,' Rudra said, making her sit on the table.

'I enjoy doing things with you and spending time with you.' Geet wiped her tears and held his hands.

'Every time you hold my hand, you give me another reason to fall in love with you.' Rudra smiled.

They promised that they would never leave each other again and would always support each other in any hard times to come. They promised to be each other's strength whenever they felt weak, to be each other's voice whenever they wouldn't find words. They promised to love each other no matter what.

As they walked together around the campus and reached the car, everyone was shocked to see them together again. Shibani saw them as she headed to the lecture room, but instead of feeling insecure, she was happy for them.

Rudra and Geet spent the entire evening loving each other. Geet was ecstatic having found the love she had lost a few days ago. She felt like she was everything to Rudra and that was the best feeling she could ever have. As he parked the car at the hostel gate, they looked at each other.

'You know, I had a dream last night,' Rudra said, coming closer to her.

'Seriously? You too were in my dreams last night.' Geet leaned closer to him.

'I saw that we bought a villa here in Goa and we were sitting on the beach facing the sea,' Rudra said, kissing her cheeks.

'Oh my god, and I saw you drowning in that sea,' Geet laughed.

'WTF. Get lost. Bye.'

Geet couldn't stop laughing for the next few seconds, but leaned forward once again and added, 'I saved you and we made out in the sea.'

Geet winked at him and her naughty smile smoothed over his feelings. Rudra gently pulled her towards him, kissing her with wild abandonment. Their bodies were locked together and they felt like they were in heaven. Rudra sucked her lips, smudging her lipstick until he felt satiated and then, after bidding each other farewell, Rudra headed back home. As soon he got there, he sent her a message:

> *Sometimes I feel lost and out of touch with reality but when you hold me, I feel safe. I could sit here and try to tell you just how I feel; only, I can't find the words. I am happy that we met and have managed to stay together after all that we have gone through.*

Rudra was fortunate to have found a girl who loved him unconditionally. After all, a girlfriend who never gives up on you is the best girlfriend in the world. Geet, too, felt blessed to have Rudra in her life as not only her love but also her true soulmate. Every girl has a best friend, a boyfriend and a true love. But she is really lucky if they're all the same person.

Not All Men Are the Same

With Tushita's intense workout that she had to religiously follow in the presence of Vivaan, her feelings for him intensified. As the strength of her legs increased, the bond between the two also strengthened. The more workouts they performed together, the more time they spent together. Every day, Tushita fell more and more in love with Vivaan. The pain and the stress made her tiresome and irritable at times but Vivaan never gave up on her. It was not easy for her but it was the only option. Tushita's leg movements were better. Her extensive workout and intense dedication was to fight for her old level of mobility and that required sacrifice. She needed to push her body to its maximum. When it became unbearable, Vivaan kept her in high spirits with the hopes of being able to walk again.

'Just ten more, come on. You can do it.' Vivaan pushed her to exercise more

'It's hurting, Vivaan,' Tushita protested as she pushed her legs upward.

'Don't complain about it. You have to walk once again and this is the practice required. Only five remaining. Push.'

'Aahhhh!'

'Excellent . . . one more . . . go . . . push . . . yes.'

'Fuck man, I will die!' Tushita screamed as she pushed for the final time with extreme pain and no strength left at all.

'Well done, my girl.' Vivaan patted her on the back and handed her a napkin and bottle of water.

Tushita looked at him and smiled, wiping the sweat from her face. As she drank the water, she stared at Vivaan, wondering how someone could be so nice. Vivaan caught her smiling and when he raised his eyebrows quizzically, she ducked her head in embarrassment and to cover it up, she said, 'If I push any more, I will have a baby.' They both laughed at the joke and then Vivaan said, 'Jokes apart, you should go to the doctor within a couple of days to assess your recovery and progress.'

'There is no need,' Tushita said.

'There is. If you don't go with Shibani, then I will take you, but you must go. There is good movement in your legs and we should ask the doctor about his opinion.'

'But why? I don't want to go to any doctor. You are a fine substitute. Anyway, I don't want to go with Shibani,' Tushita said, annoyed.

As they discussed it, they were not aware that Shibani was overhearing their conversation from a distance. She had come there to hand over the keys to them as she was going out but when she observed the care and attention Vivaan was showering over Tushita, she felt happy and her rage for Vivaan subsided. Tushita meant the world to Shibani and when she saw Vivaan's concern for her, she felt good. She had never really paid attention to Vivaan before but today she was relieved that someone else also cared so much for Tushita.

'I don't know how you will take this but frankly, Shibani was not wrong in her own way,' Vivaan offered his point of view.

'Are you drunk?' Tushita was surprised.

'I have thought about it. I know people say that being gay is a choice but that's not true. You are attracted to men the same way a straight girl is attracted to a man. It's never is a conscious decision on your part. Similarly, it isn't a conscious decision on Shibani's part. It's like asking a straight man to suddenly start liking men. Is he going to do that? Or if I suggest you to start developing feelings for girls, will you? No!'

'But how can she just . . . and Geet? Tushita stammered.

'I can understand how difficult it must be for her to face everyone. At least she had the courage to accept her sexual orientation. She even accepted that she was wrong when she took advantage of Geet's vulnerable and drunken state. No one knew about the first time they became intimate, right? There was no reason for her to confess. You probably would have still loved her. Whatever happened with Geet was an aberration. We should not make her feel so guilty. After all, she is your sister and she has always stood by you even thought you went against her advice to meet Andy. When you were bedridden did she leave you? If she didn't abandon you, then how can you not support her when she cannot even think straight?'

Tushita had no answer. She felt that Vivaan's words made sense. Some feelings are not developed on purpose but they still end up engulfing you. Just like Tushita was attracted to Vivaan and had no control over her feelings regardless of what Vivaan felt, she realized that Shibani was attracted to girls and had no control regardless of what the other person felt. She even realized that Shibani didn't force the other person to develop the same feelings for her or be like her. She had just accepted her homosexuality. As they continued their discussion, Shibani overheard everything but at one point she felt the urge to go and talk to them and that's exactly what she did. Tushita and

Vivaan were taken by aback when they saw Shibani in front of them.

'I heard what you were discussing,' Shibani said quietly.

Both Vivaan and Tushita looked at each other, not knowing how to react. Tushita sat there expressionless while Vivaan got up and stood beside Shibani.

'Let's walk, if you don't mind,' Vivaan suggested.

Shibani nodded and they walked together as Tushita sat there on the bench thinking about what was going to happen next. There was already too much confusion and complexity in their lives and she feared one more would make life unbearable. The purpose of a friendship is not to have someone who completes you but instead it is to have someone you can share your incompleteness with. Vivaan wanted to give that purpose to his friendship with Shibani by supporting her unconditionally.

'I don't know where to start but since you have come to terms with being a lesbian, I see a lot of changes in you and in the people around you. For the time being, I want to talk about you,' Vivaan said confidently.

Shibani just turned her head towards him and nodded, indicating that he should proceed.

'I assume that you feel guilty about your sexual orientation. I am just making a guess based on your general demeanour nowadays since I have never seen you like this before.'

'Let's sit with Tushita. She is alone,' Shibani said as she looked back at her sister, who was still staring at them.

'Okay,' Vivaan said, and they started walking towards Tushita.

'Yes, so what were you saying?' Shibani added.

'I think you feel guilty. You were a confident, fearless and independent girl but since your sister and friends aren't rallying around you, you seem a bit down,' Vivaan said as they sat beside Tushita.

Tushita was listening keenly.

'In life, the most important thing is love. Love can be practised by anyone, and has little to do with sex, although sex does become a major part of most people's lives. We are not just sexual beings, we are human beings and I understand that being a lesbian may not be your choice; it's just that you naturally feel attracted towards girls and there is nothing wrong with that. You are not committing any sin. Some people might think it is but remember that these people are just following what's been written down in a book that has been translated hundreds of times. Some people don't understand that being something other than straight isn't a choice, and it's been a constant thing since the beginning of time. Sin is a deliberate violation of the rules of love, truth and goodness. You are honest and loving in your relationships towards your friends. I am sure Tushita will agree with that.'

Vivaan looked at Tushita.

'Yup,' she mumbled.

'Sex is a temporal reality. In our eternal life, we will not be sexual beings, but the love that we create and share in this life will last an eternity. Among all your dealings with others, love matters the most. Sex is secondary—and optional. I asked myself: when you revealed yourself, did I make a decision to be heterosexual instead of homosexual? No. If Tushita, Geet and I didn't make a decision to be one, if we never chose for ourselves, then why should we believe that you made a decision? And so what if you did? Ultimately, it is your life. If you're not harming anyone and being honest about it, then you're doing nothing wrong. I am proud that you were brave enough to confess it openly because people rarely feel comfortable enough to do it.'

'I wanted to be true to my friends and my sister . . . but I also did not know about these feelings for sure,' Shibani responded in a surprisingly polite tone. All she had wanted was someone to understand her and Vivaan was the only one who had.

'Believe me, you are not wrong. Absolutely not! Most people are right-handed; does that make left-handed people abnormal? No! Not everyone is the same. We are all unique,' Vivaan said.

It's not what you look like or whom you like but who you are and what you do that makes you beautiful in another person's eyes. Shibani felt good because of the way Vivaan had spoken to her—he had made her feel confident about her decision. Tushita felt sorry for her behaviour. Vivaan had gradually slid into the good books of Shibani and had made her believe that not all men were the same. She was filled with respect for him. You just need one righteous and trustworthy man to change the outlook caused by bad experiences. As they went back towards the room, Tushita opened her diary and started penning down her thoughts:

When I was a little girl I would always dream of my hero. He was a fantasy that seemed perfect. My hero was strong, loving and beautiful. As I grew up, I never dreamed that I would actually find my hero, until I met you. How wrong was I when I had believed my earlier relationship to be my dream, when instead it was just a cruel truth?

But Tushita's prince is real. He is everything Tushita has dreamt about. Every little detail, every little perfection she ever hoped for is personified by him. He is not a product of her imagination, he is real. How did she get lucky enough to find the man of her dreams? She feels a deep connection with him. Today Tushita's prince brought her closer to her sister again. All the grudges disappeared with just one hug and all the tears of happiness that rolled down their eyes acted like a magical antidote for their bruises. She couldn't help but believe that his presence in her life had a divine nature. Tushita's sister and her prince had also shaken hands to finally end their long fight. Tushita was very happy to see her sister was her same old confident self once again. Tushita's family was now complete. To her, he was her perfect hero and much, much more.

'I am sorry for the way I have treated you till date. I was completely wrong in judging you based on Andy's behaviour. You are a good person,' Shibani said as she stood with Vivaan outside the hostel room door.

'We should be thankful to the warden who allowed me to be here otherwise it wouldn't have been possible.'

'I think Tushita has done very well with your help. I will take her to the doctor tomorrow for a follow-up. I can see that she is feeling much better,' Shibani said.

The door was slightly open and Tushita saw it from inside when she had gone to keep her diary on the table. She went closer but when she saw that Shibani and Vivaan were talking to each other, she decided not to interrupt them.

'Of course, she is. Her movements are much better now. Actually, I did nothing. She was charged up herself with the hopes of walking again. I just pushed her with routine gym exercises that I do on a regular basis anyway,' Vivaan said.

'Stop being so modest. Your effort was huge. I don't know how to thank you for them.' Shibani shook hands with him.

'You don't need to. It was my job. After all, you helped me to pay my college fees.'

Tushita could hear their conversation clearly and was confused about what payment they were talking about.

'That is nothing compared to the effort you put in. I am also very thankful to you for supporting me. I thought I had lost her forever when I confessed.'

'Don't worry, I won't charge you for that. You have already paid for my entire year's fee in return for Tushita's care. So, ending your dispute is complimentary from my side.' Vivaan had a wicked smile on his face.

They said goodbye and then Vivaan left.

Tushita was still near the door and she had heard every word. Her heart was pounding and her world was falling apart. She wished she could kill herself that very moment. She had fallen in love with Vivaan and had made him her prince and she couldn't bear to think that he was just carrying out a job. She wished she could hide her heart in a dark, forgotten corner where no one could harm it. She just couldn't control her tears. His care for her was not real.

It was work, something he had been paid to do. She was the only one to be blamed for being naïve enough to build the palace of her dreams.

As Shibani entered the room, she saw Tushita sitting on the wheelchair with shivering hands and her body shaking in fear and shock.

'Whatever I heard . . . is it true?' she demanded to know.

Shibani went to hug her but Tushita pushed her away.

'I hired Vivaan to take care of you because I wanted you to stand up once again. I wanted you to live once again.'

'Di . . . I don't know what you wanted but I can never stand up again. You wanted me to live but you have killed me from within. I am a dead soul in front of you. Why did you have to do this?' Tushita broke into tears.

'I just wanted to help you . . . Don't cry, please.'

Tushita ordered her to keep quiet and leave her alone. Her heart continued to beat inside her chest but her heartbeat was just functional. Vivaan didn't break her. She was already broken. He had just reopened a thousand painful scars and let all that hurt back into her life. She tried calling Vivaan but to no avail. He didn't pick up. After repeated attempts, she sent her a message:

You are even worse than Andy and I hate you for that. I never thought that the day would come when

I would hear something like this about you. I didn't believe it. I still can't believe it. I hate myself for that. Now I feel that I am not worth anyone's love. Not even the Almighty that left me with broken legs. I was well on my way to recovery but because of you I am back to square one. I don't understand how you could do something like that to me, your best friend. You led me to believe that you were caring for me out of the goodness of your heart when all the while it was just a job for you. I don't know if I will ever understand how you could have been so heartless but that's something I will deal with my own. Thanks for manipulating me along with my sister.

Hearts are as fragile as glass. They break into a million pieces. If you are afraid of falling, then you shouldn't sit too close to the edge because there could be someone waiting for you to fall into a trap!

Shut Up, Suffering, Let's Break Up

Tushita was absolutely wrong about what she had thought about Vivaan and now she was left with nothing but tears and wounds that refused to heal. She expected a reply from Vivaan for her message and when she saw him online on WhatsApp, she couldn't resist messaging him repeatedly, urging him to reply. She finally succeeded.

> Vivaan: *You can't force me to stay in your life when all I want to do is to leave. Shibani has told me everything and has paid my college fees too.*
> Tushita: *I thought you were a friend. I didn't expect you to hurt me like this. Andy used to give me physical pain and you are giving me mental pain. What's the difference?*
> Vivaan: *Nothing at all. The only difference is during that time you were physically fit but now you are good for nothing—a handicap that can't do anything alone.*

Tushita: *Oh really . . .*
Vivaan: *You have no value in anybody's life anymore. The only difference between you and an empty folder in a computer is that the folder can be deleted when not needed but you cannot be as you have become an infected virus. So don't infect us, especially me, anymore.*
Tushita: *Fuck off you loser. I don't give a damn about you. Get lost.*

Furious, she threw her mobile against the wall and it broke into pieces. Shibani was sleeping and Geet had gone out with Rudra. Tushita was hurt and was fighting the battle of loneliness alone. Whenever she thought it was love, she was always slashed into pieces. How would she mend her broken heart when there was no hope left? She flipped through the pages of her diary, reading about her prince with tears in her eyes and pain inside her heart:

Tushita was mistaken. Tushita's prince was not a hero but pretended to be one. Every smile, every step, every word had given a direction to Tushita's life but now none of it meant anything. Her life, her plans and her future with her prince had been shattered. The words that Tushita's prince uttered expressed a flood of emotions in which Tushita's palace drowned. She felt like she was standing in a room of mirrors, and all her reflections stared at her as she whirled and twirled desperately wondering what was happening to her. The reflections seemed like they were laughing at her, blaming her for jumping to conclusions. The only way out of the room was to kick out at the illusions. The heart with endless wounds holds the strongest and the powerful soul of the universe. As Tushita learned to bleed her emotions in a dark secluded room, her eyes turned beautiful. Each tear she shed taught her important lessons. Her tears had come from an unseen world to reveal something about her that she needed to work on. They told her to sit alone and have a long chat with herself. She discovered herself in silence. She understood what was missing in her life. Initially, she thought her prince was missing but when she discovered, she realized she was missing her sense of self. It was time to start loving herself more. She decided to not give up but continue on the path of recovery even if that meant doing it alone. She decided to not give up but to smile on this road to self-discovery. With or without her prince, Tushita decided to not give up and walk on her own feet, which would hurt her tremendously, but that pain would give her a new lease of life, a life in which she would love herself and smile. With or without a prince, Tushita decided to move her legs and take a step ahead in her life.

Tushita shut her diary and took a deep breath, making up her mind that she would walk. She didn't care if it was out of anger or frustration. She had discovered a well of self-belief inside her. Fear engulfed her mind as she took a deep breath. Fear of whether she would be able to walk without help. She took another deep breath and held the sides of the wheelchair firmly with her hands and applied all the pressure and strength she possessed. She lifted her lower body and eventually her legs. She fell down on the chair. She picked herself slowly once again and held the sides firmly with her wrist supporting her weight. She pulled herself upright and this time stood on her own feet with the support of the table. Her legs shook in the beginning but eventually stabilized. She didn't move but stood there. The mirror was right in front of her and she lifted her eyes to look at herself in the mirror. She was seeing something unbelievable.

She was standing on her own feet. Though she was taking the support of the table, after so many weeks she was finally standing on her own feet. She has done something she never thought she would be able to do. Tushita was awestruck. She relaxed in the same position as she felt more confident. She hadn't been cured completely but she was well on her way after listening to her inner voice. All she needed to do was to open her heart to possibilities. All she needed to do was smile in self-discovery because nothing is lost when you accept yourself.

Tushita had felt lost before but now she felt confident. She might have felt like she was drowning in the beginning but now she was diving deep into life without any fear or any expectation of a prince by her side. She had defeated the anchor which tried to pull her down. Looking at her reflection in the mirror, she smiled because she was aware that she had done something extraordinary.

Meanwhile, Shibani woke up and was mesmerized when she saw Tushita standing up. She thought she was dreaming. She was so happy for Tushita that at that moment she felt like dancing in excitement. She immediately picked up her mobile and clicked her photograph without her noticing and then went to join her. She was speechless and had to pinch her arm to convince herself that it was not a dream. Yes, it was real. Tushita was standing and Shibani's happiness knew no bounds. Tears of joy rolled down her face as she hugged Tushita. Tushita however stood without moving and did not hug her back.

'Fuck, baby, fuck . . . I still feel like I am dreaming. You finally did it. You did it, my girl. I have been waiting to see this for so long and today it has happened. I thank god for this day. Damn, I just can't stop smiling. This is crazy. I love you.' Shibani expressed her joy.

'Di . . . please. Stop with all the acting. You shouldn't thank god. You should thank the person you hired for this work. You just sold my soul.' Tushita was annoyed and pushed Shibani away.

Tushita's anger stemmed from her sense of betrayal. Of all the people in the world, the two who she trusted the most had treated her like a patient who needed to be looked after, nothing more. Controlled trust is never genuine and genuine trust requires no control.

Shibani started laughing loudly.

'What the hell do you think of yourself? Do you have no shame, laughing like that?' Tushita asked angrily.

'My little princess. You are too innocent and that is the reason why anyone can fool you very easily.' Shibani pulled at her cheeks affectionately.

'Is this sarcasm?' Tushita asked, expressionless.

'No, not at all. I truly mean it. Vivaan was absolutely right. He knows you in and out, it seems.' Shibani continued laughing.

'What?' Tushita was understandably confused.

'Yes, he was right. We fooled you. Vivaan didn't ask me to pay for his college fees, neither have I paid them. It was a trick to give you the much-needed push to stand on your own feet,' Shibani explained as she held her shoulders with both hands.

'What? Are you kidding me?' Tushita asked, completely shocked.

'When Vivaan expressed his feelings about my homosexuality in front of you and when we returned to our rooms, you were writing your diary. Vivaan and I were standing outside at that time and he gave me this idea to boost your motivation through a negative kick. I was not sure if it would work but he convinced me to give it a shot. I was bit worried but I decided to go along with it,' Shibani revealed.

Tushita stood there silently and just stared at Shibani in shock. Shibani made her sit in her wheelchair and continued, 'He was right. Initially, we thought that we had made a mistake as you were completely broken and didn't react the way we had expected you to. Yet, here you are, you were standing all by yourself a second ago!'

'So you didn't pay his college fees?' Tushita muttered.

Shibani just shook her head and laughed. Shibani immediately messaged Vivaan and sent him Tushita's picture in which she was standing. Tushita called Vivaan but he didn't pick up.

'Why isn't he answering my call?' she asked Shibani while she was getting ready for college.

'He is in his class. He hasn't seen my message yet. He will dance with joy when he sees it. I am meeting him after the class. Don't tell Geet yet, we will surprise her later,' Shibani said.

'Hmm,' Tushita said softly, still confused.

As soon as Geet entered the room, Shibani left for college. Neither of them exchanged any words or even greeted each other. Geet asked Tushita if something was wrong as she was sitting very quietly. Tushita simply shook her head. However, she was blown away with Shibani's words and was not sure if she was supposed to believe it or ignore it. Just when she had made up her mind to ignore it, she got a message from Vivaan:

Hey. Just received the picture from Shibani. Super like for it! I am not going to apologize for my act as it gave you the final boost that was needed. You must be wondering if we are lying again or if this is actually true. Yes, it is completely true and whatever Shibani told you is true. We did this just to see you stand on your own feet and you did! If I could do exactly what I wanted to right now to express my happiness, I would shout out loud in the middle of the class and moonwalk on the head of this bloody bald professor who is annoying me to no extent. This evening we will celebrate and there is a surprise for you, too. Just wait and watch. ☺

Tushita blushed and replied that she would be waiting for the surprise. She felt alive once again and as she lay on the bed, she thought:

Tushita's prince didn't let her fall on the ground when she fell from the edge. He was there to hold on to her. Now Tushita wants her prince to hold her forever. When they would meet next, her prince has promised a surprise but he doesn't know that even Tushita has something for him. She is going to confess her love for the first time, waiting to be loved right back.

The distance and time spent away from him had only made Tushita more certain that she wanted to spend her nights by his side and days in his heart. Life indeed makes sense when you find that one man who completes you. All past experiences simply feel like they moulded you into a girl who was made to love this man forever.

'Vivaan, we finally did it! I am so happy. Thank you so much. I will always be grateful to you,' Shibani said, hugging Vivaan when she met him on campus.

'She is close to me, too. Don't thank me. I cannot express what I am feeling right now. I wish I was there in that moment to witness her like that.' Vivaan hugged her back.

'I am going to buy a walking stick for her while returning to the hostel. We need to wean her off the wheelchair. It will be good if she starts practicing walking with a stick now,' Shibani said.

Both of them were delighted for Tushita and spent some time chatting with each other. Vivaan spoke of Geet after some time because he wanted Shibani to end her grudges with her, too. He wanted them to be friends again. He tried to convince her to make up with Geet, 'After all, you are friends. There shouldn't be ego clashes and there is no harm in saying sorry since you know you were out of line. Your approach towards Geet and Rudra was not acceptable. You should not lose a good friend. I am sorry if I am interfering too much but I just had to say this.'

'I know I was wrong and I have apologized but she doesn't want me to be in her life anymore.'

'I have already talked to her. She is okay with it,' Vivaan smiled.

'When?'

'Before she left for the hostel we discussed you and your friendship and I explained to her the same way I explained things to Tushita. She is okay with it and she loves you too. Ahem! Only as a friend,' Vivaan teased.

'Those last few words were not needed,' Shibani said in mock anger.

'She doesn't want to lose you. She is ready to accept you the way you are,' Vivaan said as he held Shibani's hand, trying to comfort her.

'But what about Rudra?'

'He was with us too; both of them have no issues at all. I am planning for all of us to meet together in the evening somewhere. Some nice place that is not crowded because Tushita should be comfortable there,' Vivaan said, playing with his mobile on the table.

'Great! Let's fix the place. You haven't told Geet anything about Tushita, right?' Shibani asked.

Vivaan shook his head. He was very excited about the evening. More than a party, it was a reunion of all the friends who, despite staying under the same roof now, seemed lost in their own lives. It was a celebration for the couple that made it all the way despite facing hard times. It was not less than a festival for the girl who had beaten all the odds to recover and to stand on her own feet. It was a beautiful time for the girl who had bravely confessed her feelings despite knowing how society would treat her. Everyone has baggage. If you're lucky, you'll find someone who is willing to love you enough and to stand there with your baggage and help lighten your load.

Etc—Eternal Trustworthy Companionship

Friendship is not about the rules you set for each other; it's about love, commitment, respect, trust and the fact that you do not give up on each other. Everyone had decided that they would not give up on each other and accepted each other the way they were. Rudra had zeroed in on a shack on Candolim beach where they could all meet, since it was a relatively quiet place. Rudra and Geet had come directly from college, reaching before everyone else. They sat together in a secluded area. Geet was clicking their selfies.

'How do you manage to smile so naturally?' Geet asked.

'When you're with me, I don't have to force a smile,' Rudra said, leaning over her. 'With you, it's different. You are the only one I have ever spent this much time with,' he teased.

'Oh, really, and if you had the chance?' Geet pinched his arm.

'Getting a lot of girls isn't something to be proud of. Keeping one happy is. The truth is, even if I could be with anyone, I'd choose you, every time,' Rudra added as the gap between their lips shrunk.

The moment before you kiss is more seductive than the actual kiss. This is the time when the heart is fluttering and there are butterflies in your stomach. The taste of her lips was a temptation he couldn't resist. The kiss was filled with fire that burned passion and love into every part of her body.

'Let's fulfil our fantasy of making out on the beach in daylight with the fear and excitement of getting watched by someone.' Rudra winked.

'Yes and then running naked if cops come searching for us.'

'Maturity lies in having sex without any strings attached.' Rudra smirked.

Rudra began kissing Geet from head to toe. The effect on her was electric. A thousand things he never thought he would feel raced down his spine, like a symphony.

'Every time we're together, there's nowhere I would rather be. Your smile after a kiss can light my whole heart.

I love every inch of you and it scares the shit out of me,' Rudra confessed.

'I love you. All I know is when we kiss, hug, hold hands and spend time together, I know that I truly love you more and more with every passing minute.'

There was no space for insecurities, jealousy or disrespect for each other in their relationship. Why would there be? Geet always wanted someone who didn't need to say that he loved her for her to know it was true. Rudra always proved it true. He fought for her, stood by her and made her believe that he wanted this relationship more than anything else. He made her feel that she was worth fighting for. They were not afraid of losing each other because they knew they treated each other the right way. The difference between liking someone, loving someone and being in love with someone is like the difference between for now, for a while and forever.

Rudra and Geet were now tagged in a relationship forever as she had swiped right into his heart!

A short while later, Rudra and Geet were about to sit down at the table in the shack when they saw Shibani and Tushita entering. Geet couldn't believe that Tushita was standing on her own feet with a walking stick in her hand to support her body weight and had a wide smile on her face. Geet began jumping with joy. Both Geet and Rudra went running towards her. Rudra, too, had a big smile on his face. All of Tushita's well-wishers surrounded her. She had now overcome all obstacles. Every time a wave pounds on a rusty stone, it tells it how worthy it is and each time it strikes a new melody. Vivaan was that melody of her rusty life!

'Oh my god, oh my god . . . this is crazy! You have made me so happy! Now I understood why Vivaan wanted to celebrate. He knows it, right?' Geet said in excitement.

'Yes. He is the one who made it possible. There are no words to thank him,' Tushita said.

'It's all your willpower and his dedication towards you. You are really lucky to have him in your life,' Rudra continued.

'Where is he? The host is running late.' Geet checked the time on her mobile.

Tushita told her that he was on the way with a surprise. She placed her stick beside her and sat on the chair slowly with Shibani's help. As Tushita sat on the chair, she had no hope that Shibani and Geet would ever speak to each other again, but they looked straight into each other's eyes waiting for the other to start a conversation. That's when Shibani broke the silence. 'I am really sorry for my behaviour. I shouldn't have done that. I am sorry for taking advantage of you. Please forgive me for that. It won't be repeated,' Shibani pleaded.

'I am sorry for the way I treated you. I was taken by surprise and I didn't know how to react. Then the differences between us started increasing and at one point I thought it's too late. Even before Vivaan had made me understand your position, I felt that you were not wrong. Sure, you made a couple of wrong choices, but I appreciate your courage to speak the truth and accept you wholeheartedly,' Geet said.

They hugged each other.

'Now that's more like my girls. The three musketeers are back once again,' Tushita said with enthusiasm.

True friends are a powerful factor when it comes to a happy life and all three of them had found happiness in their unconditional friendship.

As they ordered drinks, Shibani felt grateful that everyone had accepted her eventually.

'I wish that being open was easier, that people weren't either homophobic or judgemental. I was scared to tell you all because I was afraid of being rejected; I thought long and hard before I could admit it to myself and to you all. If only it was easier to say, "I'm a Lesbian and I'm proud." I know there are people out there who won't understand, but I feel strong now with you all by my side. I love you all,' Shibani announced.

Shibani was not abnormal. She was not a mistake. She was neither a monster nor a sinner. She was a human and a proud lesbian. Being a lesbian didn't mean she was retarded or wanted to sleep around with every girl. Her outrage towards men too, had been diluted completely by Vivaan, who brought positivity into her life. She promised herself that she would respect men equally as Vivaan had made her believe that it takes only one man to prove that not all men are the same.

However, that didn't mean she wanted to change herself. It's perfectly okay to be homosexual and she was up for it. She was a lesbian, she loved herself, and she loved being a lesbian!

'Here he comes, the man of the hour,' Geet said as she saw Vivaan entering the shack.

'You are late, Mr Host,' Shibani complained loudly as he walked towards them.

Tushita's heartbeat sped up as she thought of confessing her love to him. She loved him simply because she had decided to do so, with no regrets. Gradually, she got up from the chair, walking stick in hand. The moment Vivaan saw her standing, he ran to her without giving a damn about the people around. He had beautiful bouquet of flowers in his hands that he handed over to Tushita. For few seconds he silently gazed at her from head to toe. He was overwhelmed and held her by the shoulders and looked deep into her eyes. He had no words to express his joy and just hugged her tightly. Sometimes all we need in life is that one special person who deeply inspires us and gives us the courage to be who we were meant to be.

'We did it. Nothing can beat this moment. The moment that I have waited for since we started. This is captured in my heart forever. I am so happy for you,' Vivaan said.

Tushita was extremely nervous. Vivaan was the man of her life. When you are sure about the person you want to spend your life with, you want that life to start as soon as possible. She crossed her fingers and decided that it was the right moment to express her feelings but was not able to speak a word. Tushita closed her eyes for a second, still enjoying the warmth of Vivaan's arms and as he released her, she worked up the courage to finally speak up, 'I know it may sound a little weird but I want to tell you something.'

'What?' Vivaan asked looking into her eyes.

'You are the person I have been dreaming about all my life. Since the day I met you, I knew you were going to be special in my life. I felt incomplete without you; you have given me support and guidance when I needed it. I feel stronger when you are around and confident enough to take on any hardship the world may throw at me. I think you make me complete and it's because of your love that

I faced all the problems of my life so easily. I sometimes get scared thinking about what I would have done without you. Though it may sound lame, it is true. I feel like my life has lit up since you have entered it. I have been totally transformed by you. When I feel your gaze upon my face, and your hand holding mine, a wonderful feeling envelops me. Your love has turned my life around. I can't guarantee a flawless relationship, but I promise that as long as you try your best, I will be stay by your side. I just really love you. Every time I talk to you, I want to end each sentence in "I love you".'

Everyone including Vivaan was dumbstruck. Vivaan was embarrassed because he was not expecting a proposal. Looking at his expression, Tushita felt deflated and said, 'It's okay if you don't feel the same. You will still be my best friend.'

'I don't mind being your friend . . .'

Vivaan paused and Tushita looked heartbroken at that moment.

'But the reality is that you said I light up your life. So I'd rather be the bulb in your life. Besides, you cannot be "just friends" with a person you love,' he said with a big smile and Tushita blushed and hid her face in his chest.

Everyone began clapping spontaneously.

'I loved her from the day I laid my eyes on her for the very first time. My feelings never changed for her even after the mishap that happened. I was determined that my love would stand on her feet one day,' Vivaan said looking at everyone.

'I am not very good with words, but I am so glad that my actions have spoken for me. I want nothing more than to spend my life with you by my side. When I wake in the morning, I want to find you beside me. When I go to sleep at night I want to feel your arms holding me. I will be your strength holding you whenever you find it difficult to walk. I love you more than you do.'

'Now you don't even need a walking stick. He's your bulb, your walking stick, your everything!'

They all laughed, and Geet added, 'You may now kiss the bride.'

'Yeah! Kiss the hell out of her,' Shibani added.

'Do you also want me to kiss the hell out of you? My battery is always 100 per cent charged and reliable like the old Nokia phones,' Rudra asked Geet.

'Be an iPhone, dude. Show some class.' Geet laughed.

Tushita blushed as she spoke softly to Vivaan, 'I am not responsible for what will happen next. If you bite my lips or kiss my neck, I promise to rip your clothes off.'

'Damn, I really want to kiss you right here. You swiped right in to my heart, baby,' Vivaan added.

As Tushita leaned back on the table, Vivaan tasted the strawberry flavoured lipstick on her lips. Their eyes were closed and their lips transported them into another world. Ragged breathing and dancing tongues brought a fiery heat despite the cold ocean air. Desire ignited around them and they were lost in a sea of lust and love. Their kiss grew more urgent. The best feeling in the world is when you know you have found the one you love.

Champagne was called for and they all raised a toast to friendship and love. Tushita's prince had given her the confidence that she needed.

Tushita made a final entry in her diary:

> *Tushita's life is like a book in which her conscience is the author, her childhood is the prologue and the growing phases are pages filled with lessons to learn and tales of good deeds to remember. Her successes are exciting paragraphs and failures are the boring ones that she wants to skip. However, only the last chapter defines the story and until then one cannot predict the ending. Tushita had been a victim for quite some time, been used by people and had let them string her along for a long time.*
>
> *When one door closes, another opens up. Sometimes the end hurts but a new beginning is*

worth the pain. Tushita's prince had given her a new lease of life. More than the joy of walking on her own feet, Tushita was excited for her life ahead with her prince who had accepted her the way she was. Her sister, Shibani, was freed of the cage of uncertainty and was ready to spread her wings and fly in the sky with no one to limit her boundaries. Tushita's friend, Geet, had cut the ropes of fear and hopelessness with the help of Rudra and was ready to swim in the deep ocean of love. Tushita's small, loving family was now complete.

Acknowledgements

All the people I thank below were my strength while I was writing this book.

My readers for their unflinching love and support! You mean the world to me.

Jasmine Sethi, my soulmate and the only person who injects immense positivity in me and stands by me through thick and thin.

Dipika Tanna, my BFF, tagged as Rajinikanth for me and Raita Queen for Jasmine.

Zankrut Oza, for guiding me patiently and for his brotherly love.

All the people who really matter—Mom, Dad, my sister Shweta and my grandparents for believing in me.

God for being kind to me when it comes to writing.

Acknowledgements

My extended family on Facebook, Twitter and Instagram who selflessly promote the book.

Milee Ashwarya, Gurveen Chadha, Shruti Katoch and the whole team at Penguin Random House for their patience during the entire process of writing this book.

A Note on the Author

Sudeep Nagarkar has authored six bestselling novels—*Few Things Left Unsaid*, *That's the Way We Met*, *It Started with a Friend Request*, *Sorry, You're Not My Type*, *You're the Password to My Life* and *You're Trending in My Dreams*. He is the recipient of the Youth Achievers Award and has been featured on the *Forbes India* longlist of the most influential celebrities for two consecutive years. He also writes for television and has given guest lectures in various renowned institutes like IITs and organizations like TEDx.

Connect with Sudeep via his:
Facebook fan page: /sudeepnagarkar
Facebook profile: /nagarkarsudeep
Twitter handle: @sudeep_nagarkar
Instagram: @sudeepnagarkar
Website: www.sudeepnagarkar.in
Email: contact@sudeepnagarkar.in